BUTTERFLY GIRL

CALLAHAN CLAN, BOOK TWO

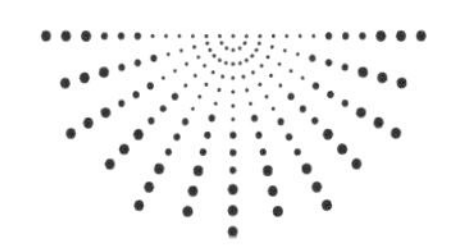

GREENLEIGH ADAMS

Lori -
Nothing like
the beauty of
a Butterfly.
♥,
GA

Greenleigh
ADAMS

This is a work of fiction. Names, characters, places, and events either are the product of the author's imagination or used fictitiously. Any resemblance to actual persons, living or dead, events, or locales is entirely coincidental.

Cover by *Wicked by Design*

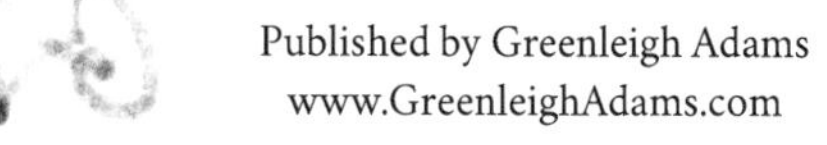

Published by Greenleigh Adams
www.GreenleighAdams.com

To all the brave women I have had the pleasure to know:
You are fighters.
Do not be ashamed of your scars—they tell the story of how you slayed the demons and won the battles.
I admire the courage it took for you to face all kinds of monsters and managed to come out stronger on the other side.
You have my utmost respect.

1

ALEXIS

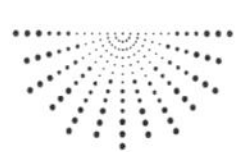

"Time of death, twenty-one eleven," Dr. Emerson stated without emotion before discarding his latex gloves into the trash can with a loud snap. I shouldn't say *without emotion*, but sometimes it appeared that way.

It was difficult to watch someone die and then move on to the next patient in the blink of an eye. I witnessed death more times than most, so perhaps I moved on easier than others. Sometimes, the transition occurred so quickly that appearing without emotion was a necessary self-preservation mechanism.

However, tonight felt different. This woman wasn't a typical emergency department patient who died due to trauma or a medical emergency. She wasn't surrounded by loved ones crying as her soul departed this earth. She was an elderly woman, probably in her eighties, who had arrived at the emergency room in full arrest with a chest-compression device strapped to her front. It was a barbaric machine that crushed the sternum one hundred times per minute to save emergency medical personnel and first responders from muscle fatigue. They no longer needed to provide manual chest compressions; they would simply attach this machine to the cardiac arrest victim and push a button.

Many people her age had a living will in place to guide their care should they have an event where they stopped breathing—or their heart stopped beating. However, she was no longer capable of making her own decisions and had no family to help, either. Without a living will or medical power of attorney, crushing chest compressions would continue if a person fell victim to cardiac or respiratory arrest.

There were no loving friends and family to hold her hand and say goodbye. She'd lived in a nursing home and never received visitors. It was probably a blessing that she didn't remember anyone or anything. Would she have looked back at her life and wished she had children? Would she have wished she had married? *I* was wondering those things, and I was only twenty-one.

It's not like I'd never met a man who showed interest in me. I certainly had. I just hadn't had any interest in pursuing any kind of relationship. I had no desire to marry and have children. At least I didn't think I did, but after this, something in me felt differently. *Is this what I really want? To die alone?*

I shook my head to rid myself of those crazy thoughts. I was barely in my twenties, not my eighties. This was *not* something I should've been thinking about. I smiled briefly at my deceased elderly patient and provided her with a little post-mortem care. I washed her face and pulled the intubation tube out of her throat.

The chest compressions had stopped, so I freed her from the device and pulled the intravenous catheters from her arms. I put a clean hospital gown on her before taking the white vinyl bag that had been placed on the stretcher beneath her and zipping up her lifeless body. I still felt a moment of sadness as the emergency room technician transported her to the hospital morgue.

"You okay, Alexis?" Charlie, my nurse colleague, asked. I wasn't facing her, but I heard her empathy-infused voice from over my shoulder. Her whispered tone dripped with concern, which raked me with uneasiness.

"Yes." I hadn't meant to clip my speech so abruptly but given my hasty one-word response coupled with turning away from her approach, she probably assumed I was discourteous. She asked if I was okay, and rather than be polite and speak to her, I walked toward the computer to complete documentation in my patient's chart. Although I'm not typically ill-mannered, I figured it was okay if I appeared that way at that moment, because I was *not* interested in having a conversation about my feelings.

I'd always been a very private person. I never shared my crap with *anyone.* I didn't have friends I confided in, and I honestly preferred it that way. I had worked the night shift with Charlie for over a year now, and although I knew she was a genuine person, I still didn't feel comfortable enough around her to share anything personal.

Most of the women I worked with were catty and shallow. They swooned over handsome men, talked about themselves, and gossiped more than tabloid magazines. I had to admit, though, Charlie was different. She was friendly and outgoing, just like all the nurses I worked with, but she didn't have perfect hair or wear full makeup at work. She was definitely into practicality over superficial perfection.

I moved on to take care of other patients—considering tonight had been slightly busier than usual. After walking out of a patient's room, I saw Charlie's brother, Cameron, enter through the sliding glass door into the emergency department holding a cardboard carrier of coffee cups. He regularly visited his sister at work. I assumed they were pretty close.

When I'd see sibling relationships, I'd wonder what it would be like to have a bond with someone you grew up with—and lived with. Knowing another person who shared the same mother and father and had the same genetic make-up seemed fascinating. Don't get me wrong, I was glad that I didn't have a sibling. Being an only child had worked out for the best, yet I couldn't help but be curious about something I'd never experienced.

Cameron had dark hair and piercing hazel eyes. Those were the prominent features I'd seen from a glimpse here and there, but I had never blatantly stared at him. He was attractive, so his mere presence made me feel a little self-conscious. However, the girls I worked with had no qualms about slowly scanning the length of his body with their eyes, drinking him in. He was certainly good looking enough... and charming, except he seemed to enjoy the attention from my co-workers a little too much for my comfort.

I attempted to observe his whereabouts without appearing like I was watching him as he proceeded to the nurses' station. As I expected, it only took a brief moment before he found himself sandwiched between Tiffany and Cecilia next to the counter. He didn't seem uncomfortable being squeezed in by two female ER nurse bookends. In fact, the wide smile he wore for those two made me believe he was enjoying himself. I tried to remain inconspicuous as I continued to survey his movements. However, once he offered coffee to the women attached to his sides, I returned my attention to the computer screen in front of me.

I didn't have my eyes glued to the electronic chart for very long before I heard him approach. I could always depend on my keen sense of hearing when someone walked in my direction, even if I wasn't looking. The outline of his figure appeared in my peripheral vision, but I heard his soft footsteps on the linoleum floor as well.

"Hey, Lex." Cameron's raspy voice resonated from behind me. I guess he was able to pry himself away from Tiffany and Cecilia—or as I called them, *T* and *C*.

I wasn't sure why he'd break away from two beautiful women smothering him to speak to me. Then again, I'd never find out if I continued to ignore him, so I decided to glance over my shoulder, not wanting to appear rude. After all, I had already given off that vibe to my co-worker. I couldn't do the same to her brother.

"Here's a coffee." Cameron handed me an insulated paper cup of hot, delicious-smelling liquid as if making a peace offering.

I wasn't used to taking drinks from men I barely knew, so I trembled slightly when accepting it. "Thank you." I wasn't sure how to behave during this transaction, so I briefly lowered my eyes before turning to face the computer again. "I appreciate it," I added, my voice laden with hesitation.

Just then, heat covered my back like a blanket, letting me know that he had leaned toward me. "Alexis, do you want to go to breakfast sometime?"

I could feel my body stiffen in a confused response to his question. *What the hell is going on? He has other women literally drooling over his presence and flaunting their assets in his face, and he asks me out?* This was all a little too much. I was the complete opposite of his type. He liked busty blondes with perfect hair and flawless makeup.

"I don't think so, Cameron. I am not much of a breakfast person." I swiveled in my seat to look at him.

"Okay. Then how about lunch?" His lips curled up in the corners as if he could wear me down with his devilish grin. Was this really happening? I had said no to a date, yet he continued to pursue me.

"Sorry, Cam, I can't." I hopped out of my seat with every intention of walking toward Charlie, who stood near the counter. Except he halted my exit when he reached out and touched my upper arm, gripping his fingers around my exposed flesh. For some unexplainable reason, I froze in place. My heavy feet felt stuck to the linoleum tiles as the warmth of his touch enveloped my entire upper body. I couldn't recall a single time I had ever locked up when someone touched me, and quite frankly, it scared me a little. *I must still be a little shook up from that older woman's death tonight.*

"Why not?"

I didn't move. The imaginary glue held me in place on the floor. The only thing I could do was give Charlie a pleading look, begging her to intervene. Obviously, I wasn't myself tonight. I never had an issue turning men down, but I just couldn't seem to form words at this moment. Hopefully, his sister could put an end to his persistence.

"Cam, leave Alexis alone," Charlie barked out with the hint of a snarl.

Relief and gratitude infused my muscles as she accepted the assignment of my rescue mission. Her support provided me the courage I needed. I mouthed "thank you" to her as I managed to find a sliver of hidden strength and propelled myself away from Cameron.

2
CAMERON

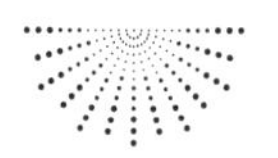

"Why are you asking her out?" my sister asked with a raised eyebrow and a clenched jaw once Alexis was a safe distance away.

"Because I like her. The same reason I ask any girl out." I shrugged as if my answer was completely obvious. I could read her like a book, but she wasn't so good at predicting what was going on in my head.

"You don't like her. She just fascinates you because she has absolutely no interest in you." She actually wagged her index finger in my direction while she spoke, which pulled a rumble of laughter from me. "She's different than the other girls I work with." Charlie lowered her voice to barely above a whisper, as if not to offend her colleagues. "She is immune to your charm."

I merely smiled and nodded at Tiffany and Cecilia, who were leaning onto their elbows braced against the counter. "No one is immune to my charm." My glance bounced from the nurses standing several feet away, squeezing their breasts together to accentuate the cleavage hidden beneath their scrub tops, back to my sister, who offered me an exaggerated eye roll.

"Have you ever stopped to think that a girl like Alexis isn't going to be interested in someone that flirts with every female in scrubs?" Her assertive attitude came to the surface as she put her hand on her hip.

"So you're saying I need to make her feel special?" I assumed she meant I needed to treat Alexis differently than a random female conquest. All this time, I didn't realize how little my own sister thought of me.

"Something like that." A nasally inhale whistled as she took in a deep, exaggerated breath in preparation for a hurtful truth. She often practiced deep breathing through her nose when she had to expel some tidbit of information that I wasn't going to like. "But she is a very nice girl that lacks the experience you have. Please, just leave her alone." I wasn't sure why Charlie was so protective of Alexis, but I had an idea how I could drive the momentum toward the direction I wanted.

"Challenge accepted." I clapped to signal that the conversation was about to be over. My sister and I had always had a competitive nature. No matter who it was against, I always wanted to win, but it was especially important when I competed against her. This was a bet I was sure to win. And because I knew my sister so well, I was fully aware that she would do everything in her power to see that I didn't. It was going to be fun.

"What are you talking about?" The inflection in her voice changed with an increasing volume. Then, after a slight glance around the area, she motioned me to follow her to the triage area in front of the department. I followed, and when we were out of earshot from everyone else, she turned around and delivered a bona fide scowl in my direction. "There is no challenge, Cameron Callahan. I have never, ever told you who you could or couldn't pursue, but that is about to change. She is absolutely off limits to you."

"Like Louis was for you?" Okay, that was a cheap shot. I lifted my brows, awaiting her response. But I wasn't past playing unfair when it came to a challenge between Charlie and me. Louis was my childhood best friend. That realization prompted my decision to add an interesting twist to the challenge. "You get Alexis to go out with me, and I will get Louis to go out with you." I extended a hand toward her.

"I can get Louis to go out with me on my own." She rolled her eyes, and I started reconsidering this idea as my hand continued to stick out in mid-air. Her sidelong glance of utter disbelief gave me the impression she was a little annoyed with my suggestion. Maybe she needed more than one date with my old friend.

"Fine. You get Alexis to go out with me, and I will get Louis to be your boyfriend."

A laugh escaped her as she dragged her gaze downward to my extended hand. "And what happens if one of us doesn't hold up his end of the deal?" Her eyebrows rose high on her forehead, expressing interest rather than the astonishment and repulsion she had just speared me with a moment earlier.

I scratched my briskly chin in contemplation with problem-solving focus. "How about a hundred-dollar wager?" The amount didn't seem unreasonable to me. I was willing to pay more than that to go out with Alexis.

"Make it two hundred." She thought I wouldn't be successful at persuading Louis to be her boyfriend. *Tsk. Tsk.* Her lack of faith in me held a little disappointment.

"That works." I accepted the terms without hesitation. Being short in confidence wasn't a problem I had.

She reached over and finally succumbed to a pump of my hand, which was still mid-air.

As she walked with me toward the exit, I could sense her demeanor change. She became too quiet, and her face clouded with uneasiness. Typically, she'd babble about how she would win any game we played, but her shoulders slumped forward, displaying a nagging uncertainty within her posture.

"Cam, I will help you with Alexis, but I want out of the deal with Louis. If Louis doesn't want to be with me, then I need to just accept that and move on." Glistening tears began to shimmer over the smokiness of her gray eyes. The water droplets hadn't crossed over the brim yet, so there was still time for me to leave without witnessing her sob. I considered myself a pretty strong man both physically and emotionally, but a crying girl tied me into an uncomfortable knot.

Recognizing that I needed to make a quick exit if I wanted to avoid any watershed, I pulled her into a brief hug. "Okay, Lean Bean. Have a good night." Then, with a few quick strides, I slipped out through the sliding glass door into the summer night before any tears spilled over.

Even though I'd met Louis first—officially making him my friend before Charlie's—the three of us had become thick as thieves ever since kindergarten. During the morning shift, the elementary school bus driver made the boys sit on one side and the girls on the other. I remembered being pretty annoyed initially because even though my sister and I didn't share the same gender, we shared pretty much everything else.

We shared a womb together, for God's sake. The bus driver wouldn't budge on the rule, even for twins, so I was forced to sit on the boys' side, and Charlie sat across from me. A scared and nervous-looking blond-haired boy had climbed the steps of the bus and walked down the aisle that first morning of kindergarten. He halted his gait and stood between Charlie and me with quiet observation.

"You can sit next to me," I said, pointing to the empty side of the bench where I sat.

"Won't your girlfriend get upset?" the little boy asked while glancing over his shoulder at my now snickering sister.

"I'm not his girlfriend, silly." Her little voice squeaked, and she playfully slapped the little boy on his shoulder. "I'm his sister."

I interrupted her quickly. "But she is also my best friend," I said proudly.

"Well, as long as she doesn't mind." Relief washed over his face.

I stood to let him squeeze past me to the seat next to the window so I could continue to sit near the aisle next to Charlie.

"We can all be best friends," Charlie offered with a smile full of missing teeth.

It turned out that Louis and I had the same teacher, and with my last name of Callahan and his being Coleman, we sat right next to each other in class.

Recess that day was so much fun. Although I made a new friend, I couldn't wait to see my sister on the playground. Those first few hours of school were the longest I had ever been away from her. Charlie happily welcomed our new friend into our time together, and the three of us had a great time playing four square and tetherball.

I was bummed about going back to class after recess, but even at five years old, I recognized that there would be many more recesses to have, so I said bye to my sister and returned to my classroom with Louis. At the end of the day, Louis and I climbed onto the school bus to head back home.

There was a different driver and considerably more kids on the bus in the afternoon than in the morning. And as I surveyed

the rows of seats, I recognized that there was no separation between boys and girls.

"I saved a seat next to me," Charlie said to our new friend and me, patting the area next to her on the bench.

Louis's eyes darted briefly in my direction before he scrambled to snatch the seat next to my sister, leaving me abandoned in the middle of the aisle. I couldn't believe he stole the seat next to Charlie. He stole the seat next to my best friend. That seat was meant for me.

But when I watched the happy grin unfold across Charlie's face once he chose to sit next to her, I couldn't stay upset with him.

Honestly, I had never been able to stay upset with either of them. They were both my best friends. So every day for the rest of elementary school, Louis and I had sat next to each other on the ride to school, and Charlie and Louis shared a seat on the ride home.

A week after my visit to the emergency room, I told Charlie that I had texted Louis. He hadn't returned to town as far as I could tell, and Charlie missed him terribly. Hell, I missed him, too. He'd been gone for five years, and I didn't think I missed him as much as I had over the last few days.

Charlie: What did you say to him?

Cameron: I asked him if he was EVER coming home again

Charlie: And what did he say?

Cameron: He said eventually...that he just needed some time to himself for a little bit.

Charlie: So how did you respond?

Cameron: I told him I understood and to let me know when he was in town again. I told him it was good to have

my friend back here. Then he just said, "will do." I haven't heard anything else since.

Charlie: Thanks for the update.

A strange, guilt-ridden feeling hit the pit of my stomach, and I had an intense urge to call her. I hadn't spoken with her in several days. I'd thought texting would be easier after the way I had acted when I saw her in the ER. But I needed to speak with her. She was technically the older twin, but I had always felt like I needed to look after her. So I found myself frantically punching the touch screen of my phone to reach her.

"Hey, Cam." At least she didn't sound pissed. Instead, her voice was cool and smooth.

"Are you okay? I mean…should I not talk about Louis anymore with you? I don't want to upset you." I wasn't exactly sure how to handle the situation between my sister and Louis, but I wanted to help.

She laughed at my comment, and I felt a rush of relief flow through me knowing that she truly wasn't upset with me. "Of course you can talk about him. He's your best friend."

"No. *You* are my best friend." I increased the cadence of my voice in an attempt to emphasize how important she was to me.

"I know. But I'm still hopeful that someday we will all be able to get past this whole fiasco and move on…as friends." Sure, I wanted that, too. But more importantly, I wanted them to finally realize what they had.

"I hope we get to that point again, too." I let out a forced sigh before continuing. "So…about Alexis."

"Cam…I'm sorry. I haven't had a good opportunity to talk with her privately." She sucked in a deep breath through the line in typical Charlie fashion like she had something difficult to say. "All the nurses I work with have a crush on you, so I don't want any of them hearing me talk about you to Alexis. If they thought I played matchmaker for my brother, they would soon all be hitting me up for a chance to go out with you." My sister always found a way to brighten my spirit and make me laugh.

"You have to fight them off me, Lean Bean?"

"As if you don't already know they are all infatuated with you." Okay, so maybe I had a clue about that.

"They are good for my ego for sure."

"You are a pig. A disgusting pig. I don't even understand why you want to go out with Alexis. She is hardly your type."

"And what is my type exactly?" If anyone could shed light on all things Cam, it would be Charlie. She was the only person who had literally known me since birth, with the exception of my parents, and perhaps my older sister, Claudette.

A stifled laugh came across the line. "You know. Blonde with big boobs."

I actually thought about her comment and took a moment to reflect on the ghosts of dating past. I guess I had never dated a girl who didn't fit that profile. Apparently, I'd made it this far completely unaware of my own pattern.

Crap. That was my problem. "I gotta go, Lean Bean. Talk with you again soon."

I rushed to end the call as I felt a wave of uncertainty pull me under. Although I always seemed to date only beautiful blondes who had considerable cleavage, I still had minimal interest in them for longer than a date or two. *If I wasn't interested in that type of woman, then why would I continue to pursue them?*

I was definitely interested in Alexis in a different way, and not just because she showed no interest in going out with me. This wasn't about a chase. I was drawn to her and needed to figure out a way to get her to see me as someone other than the flirty brother of her co-worker. *Oh, God! She probably thinks I'm a man-whore!*

The superficial types were probably okay with dating someone who had tons of conquests, but a woman that I could be serious with? A woman with depth and layers that I could take to meet my family and friends? I needed to figure out how to lose the persona I'd evoked since puberty for that to happen.

I never figured I had any inner demons, but now that they'd surfaced, I couldn't seem to shake them loose from the hold they had on me.

I wasn't sure exactly what had triggered my dive into the deep end of my soul. Maybe it was the rejection from Alexis and the realization that a woman like her would never be interested in someone like me. Maybe it was seeing how my sister and the man she so obviously loved were unable to get things right between them. *I mean, if they couldn't make a relationship work, then how could someone like me?*

I retreated into my apartment...and into my head. Maybe I just needed to talk with Lean Bean. She was my confidant, but I wasn't exactly certain what was going on with me. So it wasn't like I'd even be able to tell her. I was pretty sure I wasn't having a nervous breakdown, but then again, that thought wasn't entirely infallible.

Obviously, I had a lot on my mind. I'd been having trouble falling asleep, and when I managed to sleep, I had some very vivid dreams. Between whatever was going on with my sister and Louis and my self-reflection regarding my relationship status, it'd made for a tumultuous slumber.

I hated seeing a girl cry. I swear, when my sister Claudette cried, she always got whatever she wanted. Boys weren't

supposed to cry, so I wouldn't be able to get what I wanted very easily. Charlie didn't cry as much as Claudette, thank goodness. Then again, she was definitely tougher, braver, and stronger than my older sister.

When I walked onto the bus after my first day of second grade, Charlie and Louis were next to each other, just as they were every day on the ride home after school. Therefore, I had to find someone else to sit next to. The bus was always crowded in the afternoon, so there were very few seats left.

I shuffled my feet as I walked slowly down the aisle, eyeing the empty seats along the way. Danny Boogers, the kid who ate crunchy snot that he removed from his nostrils... No. Stinky Stanley, the kid who farted just so people had to smell his stench... No. Eats-her-hair Elise, the girl who chewed her braids... No. New girl crying in her seat... I guess that was the best choice.

"Can I sit by you?" I reflexively whispered to the little girl in an attempt to avoid scaring her in her saddened state.

She sniffled and slid in toward the window so I could sit near the aisle. No words passed through her quivering lips. Only quiet sobs leaked out of her like a wounded spirit.

"Why are you crying?" I couldn't not *say anything. "Didn't you have a good first day at school?"*

She hiccupped another sob, and the tears continued to slide down her swollen, reddened face. I probably should've sat next to the booger eater, or the farter, or the hair eater. This torture was worse, but the bus was moving, and I wasn't allowed to switch to another seat once the doors were closed.

"I like school. Kindergarten is good. I just don't want to go home." Sniffles sprinkled between her clipped words.

I wasn't sure why she wouldn't want to go home. I couldn't wait to go home. Then I could play with both of my best friends. Maybe she didn't have a best friend. Maybe that was why she was sad.

I swung my lunch box into my lap and unzipped the canvas tote. When I peered inside, I retrieved a small, wrapped chocolate bar. "You can have my Kit Kat." It was my way of letting her know I would be her friend.

She timidly grabbed the bite-size candy from my palm. A quick smile caught some of her tears in the creases, and she gave me a hushed thank you. Then, just like that, she stopped crying. That was when I had learned that chocolate made girls happy. I learned a little later that coffee made girls happy, too.

I hadn't spoken to Charlie the last several days. She'd worked three nights in a row, and two of those shifts were with Alexis. Although purposeful, not going up to the hospital to see her still felt odd. I'd brought her coffee at least once a week since she started working in the emergency room over a year ago. However, I wasn't ready to see my sister, who apparently knew things about me that I hadn't yet figured out. And I really wasn't ready to see the mysterious girl who'd had me so intrigued. I was determined to learn more about Alexis first. I had never been the type of guy who dug deep down into what a girl was truly about. Maybe that made me a jackass, but no other girl had ever held my interest like Alexis did.

Maybe it was my newfound maturity that had me yearning for more than a one-night fling, causing me to look for a girl who could offer more. And there I was with swirling thoughts again. I really needed to get ahold of myself.

Charlie would realize that I had been ignoring her, so I wasn't surprised when she texted me.

Charlie: Are you upset with me? I haven't seen you all week.

Cameron: Sorry. Just been busy that's all. I hoped she wouldn't realize that I was lying. I didn't usually lie to her. I may have withheld the truth from our older sister a time or two growing up, but I trusted Charlie with everything. She was the person I shared secrets with, even if she wasn't exactly the most perceptive person.

It was only another moment before my phone buzzed, and I saw her name and number dance across my screen again. I didn't pick up right away, which she would realize was odd for me. But I was still caught up in my thoughts, so I didn't answer her call before it went to voicemail.

Charlie: Either answer your phone or I will hunt you down. It's your choice, but you will end up talking to me.

I could tell she was serious, and she wouldn't back down, so I promptly called her back.

"Hey, Cam," she answered coolly, even though she was undoubtedly annoyed and worried about my silence toward her for almost an entire week.

"Hey, Charlie." Great. Now she would be extra suspicious. I even did a mental slap of my forehead. I didn't call her *Lean Bean*. That had been my nickname for her since I could talk. Instead of calling her Charlene, I started calling her Lean. At some point, Bean was added, and it stuck.

"Can you meet for lunch?" This was her extending an olive branch and hoping I would accept it. I hated that she felt like she had done something wrong.

"Is everything all right?" My voice hitched slightly. I was worried about her, and she was worried about me. This was typical of our relationship.

"I just want to have lunch with my brother. Is that okay?" I was so happy to have a sibling like her. I didn't get a brother like most boys wanted, but I got the best sister possible.

"Fine. The diner in fifteen?" I guess it was time for me to be honest with her. I had to tell someone what had been on my mind the last several days. It might as well be the one person in the world I could always count on.

"I'll be there." Happiness resonated from her voice. I wished she and Louis could be happy together. And I wanted happiness for myself, too.

Charlie was already seated in a booth when I walked in.

She took one look at my messy hair and the clothes I'd worn for a couple of days before donning a shocked expression. "What the hell happened to you?" No need to beat around the bush. Like I said, she was always very direct when it came to me.

I approached the booth and slid onto the vinyl-covered bench to sit across from her. "We probably should have met at my place or yours," I said after witnessing her judgmental expression over my most unkempt self.

"Are you okay?" I guess the several days of stubble on my face gave away my conflicted state.

A quiver developed in my jaw. The uncertainty of my wandering thoughts stretched out over the last few days caused a bubble to grow in my gut. I wanted to figure out what was going on with me, and maybe she could help. I clasped my hands across the back of my neck and peered upward to the ceiling. I craved her advice, but somehow, I found it difficult to meet her eyes. Continuing to stare upward, I finally spoke. "I don't know. Is this what life's about for me?"

The silence pulled my head back to its proper position, following an exasperated breath from me, once again aligning my eyes with the face of the only woman I had ever loved besides my mother. The worry on her face was completely transparent. I had always been the philosophical one, and she had always been the practical one. It seemed as though the male-female stereotypes were reversed for us, but that had always been the case. She always saw things as black and white, while I tended to see the many shades of gray. Therefore, I would have to try to explain myself to a very matter-of-fact person.

My thumbs found the bridge of my nose as I dipped forward, and my brows moved inward as I pinched that spot causing me to squeeze my eyes shut. "We're not kids anymore." I said quieter than I intended. I bolstered more strength before speaking again and forced my eyes open, even though I stared at the table while my thumbs still cradled that spot between my brows. "I'm twenty-three years old. I graduated college, and I got a job. But where am I going?" My shoulders slumped forward, though I still refused to make eye contact with her. "I go out with girls, I flirt, I have fun, but I never commit to anything serious." Silence from her side of the table surrounded me as I continued to bear my innermost feelings.

Charlie was always patient with me. I needed to get some things out, so she waited for me to continue without prodding. Thinking she might understand in a way no one else could, I felt more comfortable pulling my gaze to her and dropping my arms to my sides.

I hid my hands beneath the table as I leaned toward her, making sure I had her undivided attention. "So that's all I get in return—girls that like the way I look but aren't looking for anything serious, either." Desperate for her help, I outwardly begged for advice. "Are you going to say anything?" Pleading wasn't something I expected to do, but there I was, seeking help from the only person I trusted my heart to.

"I was waiting for you to finish." Her perplexed expression stared back at me after my confession. Usually, I exuded confidence, but today, I was showing vulnerability. I had probably thrown her for a loop, and she was unsure what to say.

"I'm finished." I searched her eyes as if she was going to shed some light on my emotional crisis.

"Cameron, you know I'm not the one to come to for relationship advice. I am obviously lacking in experience myself." Even though she was going through a relationship dilemma, I certainly didn't consider her inexperienced in the love category. She was a female, after all.

"I have been feeling on edge lately." More like anxious, afraid, uncertain, restless, and a whole slew of other adjectives that meant uneasy. "Why won't a nice girl go out with me, Lean Bean?" I couldn't hold back any longer, so I just blurted out what I had been reflecting on for too many hours to keep track of by this point. With the instant realization of what I'd divulged, I quickly raked my hands through my hair as our server appeared at our table.

"Just two Cokes please for right now," Charlie said to the waitress. She merely smiled reassuringly and waved her away.

"You think I have a type that I like to go out with. But I don't. Those just happen to be the *only* girls that will go out with *me.*" I was confident, and I flirted blatantly. I almost always got women to giggle and blush at attention from me, but I discovered a woman like Alexis wouldn't give me the time of day.

"Maybe if you didn't flirt with every female in a fifty-foot radius, you would find a nice girl." Now she was just repeating what she had already said. This certainly wouldn't help my situation.

"You mentioned that before. Truly, I am just being friendly." I returned to my earlier thought. "Okay. So maybe there is some flirting, but I swear it's harmless. It's just who I am."

And quite literally, I found myself sitting on the edge of my seat, waiting to hear her sage advice.

"Then you will continue with the same pattern you have always had." I appreciated her no-nonsense approach to situations. And I could always count on her to give me an honest opinion rather than just tell me what I wanted to hear.

Rubbing my hand across my bristly jaw made me aware of how badly I needed to shave. "So how do I change?"

She didn't even attempt to hide the chuckle that escaped under her breath. "You really need to get yourself together. You're acting like a girl, and Claudette is the sibling you should go to about being a girl." She was right. Charlie always was the tomboy, and Claudette had always been the girly girl.

"Thanks, Lean Bean. You really know how to make a guy feel good about himself." I rolled not just my eyes, but my entire head.

Meanwhile, the lines around the corners of her gray eyes burrowed deeper as her grin widened. "How about I invite Alexis to breakfast with us?"

I felt a smile tug at the corners of my lips as my sullen expression vanished.

"Maybe after our shift one morning?" Her eyebrows peaked farther on her forehead.

The heavy brick that had taken refuge in my gut dissipated, leaving me lighter than I'd felt in days. I was beyond grateful for my sister's friendship. I couldn't believe I'd ever thought about *not* talking to her about what was going on with me. She understood me better than maybe I had given her credit for. My relief settled in, and Charlie easily transitioned into our normal routine.

We were best friends exchanging conversation over a meal like we had done a million times since we'd started feeding ourselves and speaking in sentences. Truthfully, we probably exchanged our thoughts with each other even before that. And just as easily as we would make plans for a bike ride or a trip to the lake for fishing, we finalized a breakfast date for the following week. My early-life crisis evaporated just as that brick weighing me down had.

3
ALEXIS

The ER always seemed to get busier every night during the summer months. Apparently, the June bugs acted foolish and made bad choices when it came to their beach vacations. Drunken wounds, surfing injuries, boating accidents, and jet skiing traumas were the norm during the warm weather in our highly trafficked tourist destination.

"Priority one head trauma coming in by chopper," Charlie said to me as I returned to the floor from my very brief break. She breezed past me and into our large trauma resuscitation room to prepare for the arrival of our critical patient. "Eight minutes to the scene, ten minutes back."

I needed to focus on the injured patient on his way, but I hadn't been sleeping well—which happened to a lot of nurses who worked night shifts. But I was pretty sure my lack of sleep was because I had a lot on my mind and not due to an alteration in my circadian rhythm.

"Alexis, you got my back, right?" Charlie continued to check supplies and equipment in the empty patient room while I stood outside the threshold.

"Of course." I nodded and shuffled my feet to assist her in

the preparation, hoping for some automatic drive to kick in and allow me to work efficiently without requiring too much thought. I wanted to help my colleague. Even though we weren't exactly friends, she was my favorite nurse to work alongside.

I was also very appreciative that she had come to my rescue from that uncomfortable situation with her brother last week. I hadn't been on a date in a very long time. I was only twenty-one, so I had my whole life ahead of me. I didn't need a man dragging me down.

Although, I also recognized that I didn't want to be alone my whole life, either. *Damn that old woman for dying last week and causing me to think about being alone when I die.* Maybe when I was much older, I'd be interested in dealing with a man, but I couldn't foresee that being anytime soon. I wasn't a man-hater per se, but I found them controlling, demanding, and selfish. Additionally, grown men would sometimes throw a temper tantrum fiercer than any toddler when he didn't get his way, and I didn't have the patience for that. I also didn't feel like having that kind of drama in my life at the moment. It was emotionally exhausting. I'd heard there were some good guys out there, but I had yet to witness any myself. I also probably didn't let my guard down long enough to find out if a guy was nice or not. I'd push them all away just the same.

The reality was that I may not have seen any good guys, but I had seen some bad ones. I had seen ones who physically tortured women too many times during my short time on Earth, which was really the true reason I'd *never* let my guard down.

"What is the mechanism of head injury? Tourist dove into the shallow end of a pool?" This time of year always had me predicting the consequences of vacationers' bad choices.

"Nah." Charlie checked the oxygen tank beneath the

stretcher and surveyed the breathing masks and cannulas while she spoke. "Some local guy beat the crap out of his wife with a baseball bat."

Bile crept up my throat, and perspiration prickled against my clammy skin. I willed the stomach acid back down, but the nausea wasn't so willing to comply with my request. I could force myself not to vomit, but I couldn't get rid of the feeling that I needed to. I always ate quickly at work because I didn't want to leave my co-workers for too long. But at that moment, I regretted my usual hasty meal since it sat like concrete in the abyss of my gut.

Flashes of unwanted recollections flashed in my mind like flipping pages in a magazine. The images were colorful, vivid, yet repulsive. In my attempt to avoid panic, I glanced at my watch and discovered I still had a few minutes before the patient would head to our hospital. I took that opportunity to excuse myself for a quick trip to the ladies' room. Making a brief stop to the bathroom before a trauma patient's arrival was actually a norm, because you couldn't predict how long you might need to be bedside literally saving someone's life. It could be hours; therefore, sneaking away to the restroom was something I felt like I could do without drawing any suspicion.

So I exited the room quietly and slipped into the employee ladies' room, pulling the heavy, wooden door shut and clicked the lock into place. Thankful for the tiled wall, I leaned against the cool surface and cursed myself for traveling down memory lane into a past I'd rather forget and never revisit. I had been pushing visions from my childhood down so far into the furthest reaches of my mind ever since high school in the hopes that those images couldn't be located again, even with GPS.

But for some reason, with one unexpected yet brief patient report, I couldn't pull my mind away from memories that had once invaded me with sadness yet now shook my body with anger. I hated that I couldn't seem to control my feelings or my mind from taking me back to a place I didn't want to go. I was a grown woman now, and I despised when I felt anything less than confident and strong. I had too often felt weak and afraid when I was a little girl, and I sometimes needed to remind myself that I wasn't that scared, vulnerable child anymore.

My thoughts reeled me back in time, but I continued to try to fight them. *I have moved on,* I recited the same chant over and over again, just as I had so many times throughout my life. Sometimes it was a silent plea, and other times, like now, I said the words loud and proud, willing the memories to leave me alone.

I always wanted to believe that coming out on the other side of a traumatic childhood had left me stronger. I relished in my accomplishments, recalling how I'd managed to work my way through college and dive into a career that I loved.

After too many years of sinking into quicksand, I managed to claw my way out of the hole that threatened to swallow me, climb a mountain, and reach the summit. I was one of the few women who could say that, so I was extremely proud of my tenacity and perseverance.

But slipping back into those weak moments in my mind caused me the same feelings of claustrophobia as those intimidating walls started to move toward me, squeezing me into a smaller and smaller space until I was completely boxed in with nowhere to flee. Unfortunately, that wasn't where it ended. Once I was rooted in a confined area without an escape, I felt sand gather around my feet and creep up my legs, immersing me until I eventually felt like I was drowning in dust, causing a choking sensation to form within my throat as I gasped for air. Normal people would call that a panic attack. But for me, it was merely an inconvenience that only periodically showed up. Fortunately, I was *always* able to combat it. I was a fighter, and even though I might've needed to remind myself occasionally, I felt confident that no one or nothing could ever hurt me again.

My biological father was physically abusive to my mom. It didn't take a psychiatrist to determine my distrust of men was a result of that. It wasn't just an occasional shove or smack, either. He was extremely cruel and took abuse to another dimension of domestic violence.

My mom had burned dinner once, so my father thought retribution came with burning her. He'd lit a cigarette and dragged the hot ember tip up and down her forearms multiple times. To make matters worse, he had no regard for performing such a heinous act in front of his daughter. The smell of burnt flesh, the blood-curdling screams from my mother, and the sight of charred skin sporadically made an appearance as a grotesque image that I could see on the widescreen of my mind with a muffled soundtrack. I understood it wasn't real, but although distorted, I could make out the memory all too clearly.

When my father—I'd never call such a horrific person *Dad*—saw her talking to the mailman one day, he punched her in the face and broke her nose so that "no man would find her attractive again." Again, the cracking reverberation causing a nasal bone fracture was a noise I would never forget. Neither was the sight of blood pouring out of my mom's nostrils like two spigots and coating her white shirt.

I could go on and on about cuts, bruises, broken bones, burns, and busted lips, but with only an occasional slip-up like what happened tonight, I was pretty efficient at keeping most of those memories buried deep inside.

When I was ten, my father had come home and said he was disgusted by my mother, so he left. He just packed up and left. I couldn't understand the sadness that surrounded my mom regarding that event. I remembered being overjoyed to have that man out of my life. I hadn't seen him since that day, and I didn't miss him one bit. I had no idea why she had stayed with him all that time, but leaving had never even been a consideration for her. Fortunately, my father had never raised a hand to me, but I saw the aftermath of what he did to her just the same.

Regrettably, she didn't stay without a man for very long. My mom began dating—too soon for my liking—in an attempt to recover from her sadness. From where I stood, I would've assumed that she'd date a man who was the opposite of my father. But she wound up dating another abusive man.

The first guy my mother dated after my dad was not so selective with his abuse. He got into fistfights at bars and lost several jobs due to his temper and anger issues. My mom moved him into our house anyway. Again, I fell witness to the same abuse, only at the hands of a different man. I had read the articles in the academic journals, and I witnessed firsthand the cycle of domestic violence. The information was all the same. A woman would continue to fall into the same relationship patterns because that was all she knew.

Additionally, her lack of confidence made her vulnerable, which allowed these predatory men to convince her that she needed him or that no one else would want her. The evidence also suggested that children who grew up in abusive homes would end up being victims themselves when they began to date. Well, that is *never* going to happen to me. I was better than that. I would just as soon be alone than in the relationships I saw my mother have.

Not only did I have the strength of mind to avoid those situations, but I also learned how to defend myself as well. I decided a long time ago that I would *never* let a man physically hurt me. The first time I had to protect myself was during my junior year in high school.

My mother's live-in boyfriend had been upset about something. I never did find out exactly what had sparked his anger, but he was in the kitchen with my mother when he began pummeling her with his fists. She held her forearms up, trying to shield her face from his punches, but he continued to wail on her. The empty thud of a clenched hand into her abdomen and the smack of flesh being split open as he struck her upper jaw were other sounds that sometimes haunted me.

I was sixteen at the time of that disturbing vision in my kitchen, and I had been living that life long enough. At that point, I'd made the decision that if she wouldn't defend herself, then I would have to step in. So that's what I did.

I yelled at him to stop, and he flinched at the screech of my voice. His nostrils flared and he glared at me, baring his teeth like an angry dog. His evil scowl didn't deter me, though. I confidently approached him, deliberately stomping my feet as I moved closer. I watched the muscles and veins in his neck strain against his skin before he drew his closed fist back and tried to take a swing at me. He was much larger than me, but I was quicker. I dodged his failed attempt at a blow to my head. Reflexively, I grabbed the largest knife out of the wooden block on the kitchen counter and waved the sharp, shiny metal blade at him.

That got his attention really quickly. His eyes widened and, I swear, they bulged out of the confinements of their sockets. He realized I wasn't scared of him. He stiffened and backed away from me, but when my mother dropped her arms to her sides, coming out of her defensive stance, he threw another swift punch to her abdomen. Acting on impulse, I jabbed the blade into his side, right through his shirt and his fatty layers of skin and tissue. I let the knife continue its path until it wouldn't go any farther. Then I removed the blade, coated with his crimson blood, and plunged it into him again.

He crashed to his knees and fell onto his back. My mother actually yelled at *me* for what I had done to *him*! She scurried to his side and screamed for me to leave. She basically told me in no uncertain terms that I was no longer welcome there. So I left. I grabbed a few things from my dresser and closet on my way out.

And that was the last time I saw her. That was five years ago, and I didn't miss her one bit, either. I shouldn't hold on to so much hatred to the people who'd given me life, but old habits die hard. I couldn't remember a time when I felt love for either of my parents, so it wasn't difficult to hold on to the only emotion I had associated with them.

I never went back to that house. I never even found out what had happened to my mom's boyfriend. I honestly didn't have a clue what had happened to my mom. I wasn't even sure if either of them was still alive, or even if they were still together. I suppose a lot of people would feel sorry for me, but I was actually grateful for how things had turned out.

I was grateful that assault charges never came my way. I was grateful that I had a car I could sleep in when I didn't have anywhere else to go. And I was grateful that I had a job so I had an income. Many sixteen-year-olds were without cars and money, so I had some things others in my situation hadn't.

I had no idea why the cops didn't show up and haul me away to juvie. I certainly could've been found because of the aforementioned car and job. I continued to go to school, as well. It'd taken several months, but I finally stopped anticipating being arrested by every police officer I saw.

It would have been easy to skip going to school. I mean, who would force me to go? I had zero adult supervision. And with no one telling me what to do, I could do what I wanted. Thankfully, I wanted to go to school. I wanted to get a degree, acquire a career, and support myself financially so that I would *never* need to depend on a man for *anything*.

Luckily, I was determined and ambitious, because I doubt anyone at my high school would've cared if I had stopped attending. It wasn't like I had any friends—which was my choice. Considering my home life, I never even wanted to invite someone to my house when I was younger. Not to mention, my life seriously sucked, so I didn't have anything in common with anyone. *What would I have talked with anyone about, anyway?*

I still had the same Honda Accord, but I didn't sleep in it anymore. I lived in a cute one-bedroom apartment now, and I had personally earned everything in it. It hadn't been an easy road, but it was the journey that had led me to where I was now. I'd graduated high school but didn't attend the ceremony. It was a personal achievement. I didn't need the celebration and accolades. Besides, everyone else in my graduating class would've been surrounded by family; I didn't have anyone I could share my accomplishment with.

Graduating high school was really only one step toward my goals, anyway. I wanted a career as a nurse, so I enrolled in a community college just prior to graduation and received an associate degree in nursing two years later. Immediately after passing my board certification about a year ago, I had applied for a job at the local hospital…and I'd been an emergency room nurse ever since.

Charlie and I had both started working at the same time. She had graduated from a four-year university, so she was a couple years older than me, but we both held the same board certification.

Drawing my mind back to the present helped ease me out of hiding in the restroom, and I returned to the empty trauma room. I expected to see Charlie, the ER physician, a tech, and maybe a respiratory therapist surrounding the stretcher, perhaps someone from Xray, too. But the room stood sterile and bare.

I searched the room for a staff member—*any* staff member—but I was unable to locate anyone.

"Crisis averted. Patient was rerouted to Baltimore due to the extent of her injuries." Charlie's calm voice relaxed that rocky feeling in my stomach, and I allowed the sensation of relief to wash over me.

Seeing the interactions with other people, I wondered if I had missed out on something because I, essentially, never learned how to make friends. I could potentially see myself being friends with someone like Charlie…maybe.

"You feel like going to breakfast after one of our shifts, Alexis?" Her friendly tone made me want to try out the friendship thing.

"Sure. I'd like that." I felt my lips stretch across my face as I gave into a smile. Friendship wasn't something I had experienced before, but maybe it was time for me to step into the world I had been missing out on.

4
CAMERON

Somehow, during Charlie's relationship crisis with Louis, she still managed to make a new friend. That's how Charlie was. She was friendly and outgoing. When we were little, Mom said she would approach random people in the store or the mall and introduce herself to complete strangers. I didn't remember that, so it must've been before we were five, which was when my lasting memory had developed. But it was one of my parents' favorite stories to tell.

Even when we got a little older, she would make friends wherever we went. At the playground, at little league games, or school, she would ask to join anyone playing. She was quite the tomboy, so she mostly approached boys. A few times she was told that girls can't play football, basketball, et cetera. But then they would see her throw the football or dribble a basketball or hit a baseball, and they would fight to have her on their team.

I made friends, too, but I had moved at a little bit of a slower pace than Charlie. ***It took me three days and an equal number of Kit Kats to ask crying girl her name. Every day, I*** *would ask why she was crying, and every day, she said she didn't want to go home.*

"I'm not allowed to tell strangers my name." She said with rivers of tears again streaming down her cheeks.

"Stranger? I'm your friend." I sat next to her on the bus, and I'd given her candy. In second grade, that's practically considered being best *friends.*

"I wish I could change my life." She sighed, and with the Kit Kat in her hand, the crying slowly began to subside. "You know like how a caterpillar changes to a butterfly? A butterfly gets to have a better life than the ugly caterpillar. A butterfly gets to fly away and see the world, while the caterpillar is stuck crawling around." She was pretty smart for only being in kindergarten.

"Well, since you're not allowed to tell me your name, I'll just call you Butterfly then." It was better than calling her crying girl, anyway. "Maybe I should have a name with wings then, too."

"You mean, like, a bird?" Her eyes grew wide and curious.

"No. I mean, like, Batman."

She let out an adorable giggle in between sniffling whimpers of her soft sobs. I couldn't believe I actually made her laugh. "Batman doesn't have wings. He has a cape."

"But he has a car that can fly, so I want to be him. We can be Butterfly and Batman. Best friends." She nodded in agreement and then locked her thumb with mine so that our fingers spread outward like wings. And at that moment, I had a new best friend.

Travis was the newest friend Charlie had decided to adopt. Technically, I was friends with him first—this seemed to be an established pattern with us. We both worked at the local high school; he was a teacher, and I was the athletic trainer. We weren't close by any means, but I had sat through enough faculty meetings and professional days with him to consider him more than an acquaintance. These events usually reverted the genders to segregate, much like middle school dances. The men sat on one side of the room, and the women sat on the other. Therefore, I sat next to him, or near him at all those events. We ate lunch together in the faculty breakroom on occasion, so I'd heard about some of his personal stuff.

I may have misinterpreted Travis's original intention regarding my sister and thought that he was looking to date her. But they both quickly learned that neither were ready to begin dating again, so they decided to be friends instead. Travis was now a regular attendee when Charlie and I spent time together. She and I still liked to catch a meal, go kayaking, go for a bike ride, or spend time at the beach. I gave her a hard time, but I considered her my favorite person. She was supportive when I needed it, but she gave me a kick in the pants when I needed that, too. We shared a lot of the same interests and hobbies, so we had a lot in common. I figured girls like my sister were one in a million, and that's why I haven't met anyone else like her. She's fun to be around and isn't afraid to get her hands dirty.

Since it was already natural for Charlie, Travis, and me to go out for a meal, having her bring Alexis along wasn't a far stretch from our norm. As Charlie had already pointed out, I was very intrigued by Alexis. I was looking forward to going to breakfast with her.

Travis and I had arrived at the diner and secured a booth by the time Charlie and Alexis showed up after their shift. Charlie thought it would be easier to convince her to come to breakfast if we ate immediately after their overnight shift. She said there would be less pressure because it would only be for a short while, and then the two girls could go home and sleep.

Alexis approached alongside of Charlie but didn't seem at ease. She crossed her arms over her chest like a comforting hug as she stood next to the table. I didn't take the gesture as an attempt to be closed off to us. I figured it was a way to calm herself before moving into an uncomfortable situation.

I wasn't going to let her stay uneasy for long. Rather than stand and have her slide into the booth being trapped against the wall, I slid toward the interior of the bench, and Travis did the same. Charlie was quick to scoot next to Travis, leaving the only option for Alexis in the spot next to me.

I swallowed hard during that devastatingly long moment while I silently willed her to take a seat on my side of the table. With obvious reluctance, her slim figure bounced on the vinyl as she finally gave in and accepted the last place at our table.

"I showered this morning." I might've mumbled that under my breath, but it didn't stop her from hearing me. She swung her pale blue eyes my way.

"If you don't want me to hear your thoughts, you might not want to say them out loud." She batted her dark-blond lashes—which may have just been her blinking, but I was mesmerized just the same. My emotions had never been swarmed with fascination and nervousness simultaneously before.

"That's good advice. I'll be more careful about my slips of the tongue." I realized what I said the same moment Travis and Charlie erupted with laughter. *Couldn't they just be good friends and ignore my blundered comment?*

But turning my attention away from the goofs across from me, I heard small giggles, and Alexis's shoulders shook with humor. Maybe I hadn't screwed up too badly if she could find the hilarity of my blooper. Her eyes sparkled with amusement, and I instantly felt more at ease.

Conversation flowed naturally, and I found myself having a great time laughing and relaxing. We talked about everything, and we talked about nothing. Alexis seemed shy and reserved at first, but she slowly began to share a little about herself. She talked about high school, and college, and work. I was enjoying our easy conversation when I caught a glimpse of my childhood friend out of the periphery of my vision standing at the pickup station of the counter. I jerked my head to reaffirm my quick observation. He stared in our direction, so I assumed he saw the group of his friends gathered at the table not too far away. I shot my arm upward and waved, drawing the attention of everyone seated near me as I motioned him over to the booth. He appeared rooted in place, so I called out to him. "Louis!"

Charlie's face lit up like a kid at Christmas. Joy shone in her gray eyes as her lips stretched into a smile. I figured she was happy to see him, but Travis didn't display the same contentment. With some hesitation on his part, Louis eventually approached our table.

"Cam told me you crashed at his place last night." Even Charlie's voice had a sunny cheerfulness. I watched as her cheeks reddened while she blushed. I had never seen her in such awe of another person on the planet. Ever. Seriously, I had seen her meet some of her favorite professional athletes without so much adoration seeping from her pores.

"I figured you would sleep in, so I snuck out this morning without waking you." I was feeling particularly content, so I exchanged a grin with my friend.

"You do have a lot of experience sneaking out in the morning without waking anyone." Great. I was doing my damnedest to convince Alexis that I wasn't an ass, and my lifelong friend was sabotaging me.

That puppy-dog expression that Charlie had been wearing since Louis approached resolved and she, not so subtly, made a gesture with her finger across her throat to try and stop Louis from saying anything more to damage my reputation in front of Alexis. She's a good sister.

"I'm totally kidding. Cameron has always been a complete gentleman." He smiled at Alexis and offered her his outstretched hand. "I'm Louis. And you are?"

So much for my friend making me look like an ass. I was doing that all on my own. I hoped I could recover from the lack of introductions. "I'm sorry. I don't have any manners this early in the morning, I suppose." I stumbled over my words. *Smooth dude. Real smooth.* "This is Alexis. She works with Charlie."

"I figured as much given the scrub costume."

Charlie exhaled a long sigh of contentment in response to his words. These two needed to figure out that they were meant to be together.

Caught up in her bliss for a beat longer, I witnessed her break free from the gaze holding onto the connection between her and my friend that was palpable to everyone at this table. "And this is Travis. He works with Cameron at the high school." Louis simply nodded in response to Charlie's comment.

Alexis grasped Louis's extended hand and pumped it in a dainty handshake. But when he turned to Travis, he only furrowed his brows and pursed his lips into a thin line.

A handshake between the two men didn't happen. The cashier yelled Louis's name, and the pair broke their death stare with each other, ending their standoff. "Well, I don't want to interrupt your double date any more than I already have, so I'm going to grab my sandwich and head out."

His attempt to establish some pleasantness became futile, as a distinct hardening of his eyes developed. He was obviously uncomfortable with the situation. I was sure he thought Charlie was on a date with Travis. I could have offered clarification, but I either didn't think quickly enough, or I figured it was best to let things play out between them. So Louis retreated to pick up his breakfast and rapidly exited the restaurant.

Following a slightly awkward day at the beach the next day with Charlie, Travis, and Louis, we planned dinner for the following week for the four of us, plus Alexis—and my other sister Claudette. I'd found it challenging to watch Charlie stare dreamily at Louis at the diner. But watching my childhood friend drool over my sister in a bikini during our beach excursion was more than a little weird. At least it seemed like Travis and Louis were able to speak to each other after our outing without the condescending glares and the mutual muscle-flexing. I tried not to think about the weird exchange that continued to occur between those two men, and I decided to focus on seeing Alexis again instead.

The previous morning at breakfast, I'd felt so at ease sitting next to Alexis. And for the first time in forever, I wanted to see the same woman a second time. In fact, I couldn't wait to just see her again. I couldn't wait to sit next to her and have her talk with me. I, unfortunately, had to admit that maybe I'd been a bit of a man whore at times. The only emotion I had toward a woman previously was most likely lust. If I wanted to see a woman again, it was to see her without her clothes on. I didn't even care if words were exchanged.

But Alexis was different. I wanted to learn things about her. I wanted to hear her voice. I wanted to see her sweet smile. I wanted to know if I could ever get her to laugh. I wasn't sure how to identify that emotion because no single word could describe it.

I got excited to see her…like, meeting-your-favorite-all-time-sports-player kind of excited. I developed a tickling sensation within my stomach, and my pulse kicked into another gear as my heart rate accelerated. Just thinking of her could induce these same feelings—I didn't even have to see her. Sure, it was a little bizarre for me to have this happen, but I didn't want it to stop. I wanted to continue to feel that way. If this was how Charlie and Louis felt about each other, I couldn't understand why they wanted to push the emotion away. I wanted to embrace it.

Louis, Travis, and I drove together to dinner the following week. We offered to take Charlie too, but she quickly declined. I wasn't sure what her latest status was with Louis, but I'd decided I would let everyone else engage in their own drama. I planned to only focus on Alexis.

She was already sitting in the lobby staring at her phone when Louis, Travis, and I arrived at the restaurant. She didn't have her hair pulled back into the ponytail I had always seen her with. She let her long, dark-blond hair flow around her shoulders for tonight. It was a beautiful look on her. Her brilliant, light blue eyes pulled upward and caught the sight of me. I'd been told my hazel eyes could be both endearing and threatening, so I didn't want to scare her off. The soft curve of her lips pulled into a gentle smile. It was merely a friendly gesture, but I somehow found it incredibly sensual. Her subtle actions made a bigger impression on me than the blatant signs typically thrown my way.

I admired her colorful floral top. It reminded me to have a bright outlook on life. It seemed like not too long ago, I was trying to go to a dark place, but her entrance into my life was like the rainbow on a sunny day following a thunderstorm when dark clouds had once filled the sky. *Lord, what is this girl doing to me?*

"Hey," I managed to say. I hadn't been nervous speaking to a girl since eighth grade. But this girl had me nearly trembling with anticipation.

"Hi, Cameron." Her voice was soft, and her lashes fluttered as she spoke. She wasn't flirting with me, but maybe that's what I liked so much. She was just being herself.

Charlie walked into the lobby after our brief moment. Alexis and I broke our short-lived re-acquaintance, and we all exchanged pleasant hellos before the hostess guided us to a six-top table in the middle of the dining room. Charlie followed me, and Louis followed behind her to fill the three seats on one side of the table. Then Alexis sat across from me, and Travis sat next to her, across from Charlie. I was happy with the seating arrangement.

But before Alexis and I could begin a conversation, Claudette flew in like a whirlwind of blond hair. "I'm so sorry for being late," she said, nearly out of breath.

My older sister quickly hugged Charlie and then kissed me on the cheek. "Hey, Claude," I managed to stammer.

"It's good to see you again, Claude." Louis stood to hug her, and she kissed his cheek also.

She made her way to the other side of the table and extended her hand to Alexis, "Hi, I'm Claudette."

"Alexis." The woman I would like to consider my girl, pumped my older sibling's hand once without standing up from her chair. They nodded to each other, and then Claude turned to Travis.

Louis returned to his seat, but Travis was standing when Claudette reached for his hand. "Hi, Claudette, I'm Travis." Rather than shake her hand as Alexis had done, he grabbed her by the fingers and brought them to his face to plant a soft kiss on her knuckles. *Gag!*

Claudette's face turned a bright shade of pink as he pulled out her chair for her. Once she was seated, he pushed the chair in and sat next to her. The two of them began a dialogue, leaving just Louis and Charlie to be forced to speak to each other. Maybe this dinner would turn out okay after all.

"It looks like everyone is suddenly paired up at this meal," I said to Alexis. I now had a close-up view of her blue eyes sparkling at me. I also had the opportunity to observe that those blue gems were surrounded by the prettiest, longest eyelashes I'd ever seen. She didn't wear that black, painted-on crap that Claudette and other girls did. I definitely preferred the soft, naked look of her lashes.

Her silent demeanor didn't sit well with me. I really hoped she would open up some more. She was more talkative the other morning at breakfast. Maybe that comment I made about pairing up was too much too soon. But considering Claudette and Travis were consumed with each other, and whatever was going on with the Charlie-Louis situation, it was going to be a very long, boring dinner if she and I didn't somehow find a way to hold a conversation.

Her lips slowly tugged upward in that adorable smile I loved to see, and she leaned forward, resting her forearms on the table. Moisture left my mouth and my pulse quickened, knowing that she was about to speak to me, and only me. "Didn't Claudette and Travis just meet?" Her gaze bounced between them and me. "They are certainly smitten with one another."

Did she really just say "smitten"? My Lord, she was adorable. "Yeah, it appears they are. Do you believe in love at first sight?" I whispered unintentionally.

"Uh...no." Her tone was louder than mine, and her gaze

immediately dropped downward, making me aware that I'd said something she didn't like. I continued to watch her eyes move up and down as if glancing over the menu for a dinner selection.

"Have you ever been in love?" I had no idea what anyone else at the table was talking about. Alexis was the only person I was focused on, and my curiosity prickled my skin. Her abrupt coolness had me wondering if someone had broken her heart before.

She looked up at me again and straightened her spine, but I still detected a pensive shadow in the depths of her eyes. "No, have you?"

I wasn't sure how to answer. *Would it be insensitive to tell her the truth?* If I had any hope of developing something with this woman, I was certain I shouldn't lie. She didn't seem like the type to forgive easily. "No, I haven't."

She shrugged casually at my comment and quickly returned to her menu.

"But I'm not against being in love," I blurted out with pressured speech. I really wanted to make sure she was aware I was looking for a more substantial relationship than the superficial ones I'd engaged in previously. "I just hadn't met the right person."

A visible shiver quickly overtook her. Maybe she was chilly. I watched the intimate movement as she brushed her hands up and down her arms, and all I could envision was my own hands moving up and down those graceful arms to warm her up. Maybe one day soon. Then again, I needed to get her comfortable enough to speak to me. Then I could work on getting her comfortable enough to let me touch her. I imagined her creamy skin was soft and silky smooth.

"Cameron, I don't want you to get the wrong idea." Her voice dropped to barely above a whisper when she leaned forward again to speak to me. "I'm not looking for a relationship."

The *"I'm not looking for a relationship"* speech typically meant the woman who said it was only looking for a fling. Alexis hardly seemed like the one-night-stand type, so I took the shot to my gut to mean she didn't like me at all. I desperately tried to regroup and think of a comment to convince her that investigating this connection was worth exploring.

"Well, how about a friendship? I'm an excellent friend." I motioned around to the others at the table. "Ask anyone here."

I was fully invested in her response. She sucked in a deep breath, and I did the same in anticipation of her reply before she mumbled, "Cameron…" through an elusive half-smile.

I huffed with enough force to cut her short before she could finish. "And my friends call me Cam. Okay, Lex?"

A sound resembling a giggle bubbled out of her, causing a weird sensation to dance in my belly. It was closer to a laugh than I had gotten from her so far. "Okay, Cam."

And just like that, maybe she would allow me to be her friend. We made small-talk while the waitress delivered our drinks and took our meal orders. She ordered a bacon cheeseburger with French fries. She was a girl after my own heart, for sure. I liked that she didn't order a salad or some other light option. My sisters told me years ago that even though girls ate cheeseburgers, most didn't order such food on a date. I was done with that type of woman. I wanted someone who could be herself around me.

I tried to remain focused entirely on Alexis, but I noticed Charlie leave the table, and shortly thereafter, Louis followed. Several minutes went by before either of them returned. I was aware of the timeframe because Lex and I had talked about my job and favorite hobbies for a while before Charlie and Louis rejoined our table. They were speaking to each other after their reappearance, so I took that as a good sign. Without having to worry about them, I could once again return my entire attention toward the beautiful woman sitting in front of me.

"Do you have any siblings?" I asked Lex while awaiting our food.

"No," she deadpanned. "Do you have others besides Charlie and Claudette?" The quick closure from her response still opened the door for a question directed at me. I loved how her eyes were wide and bright and focused on me. She genuinely appeared to be intently listening. I was not used to that at all. Most girls couldn't care less what I said or what we talked about. But Lex acted interested in me…the *real* me.

"Yeah, Louis. He isn't my brother by blood, but we grew up together, and he practically lived at my house most of my life. Besides, he's an only child, so we had to give him the experience of having siblings." I could tell she was absorbing the information I gave her. "There's not going to be a quiz later," I said jokingly to reassure her. "You don't have to take so many mental notes."

Her teeth peeked out from behind her lips, and that warm feeling returned within my belly.

"What about your parents? What are they like?"

And just as quickly as her display of contentment appeared, the color drained from her face. *Shit! I said something wrong. Were her parents dead? Had there been some tragic accident?* I had no idea what to do or say. I was pretty sure I wasn't going to recover from that comment. Words wouldn't form on my lips, and I couldn't figure out how to retract what I'd said swift enough.

"They aren't around anymore." Her cool voice twisted me in the gut. But she casually picked up her water glass and pulled a long swallow through her straw.

"I'm sorry. I didn't mean to bring up a bad subject." I felt terrible, even though I had no idea painful memories were associated with her parents. Now I was the one who needed to make mental notes.

Placing her cup back onto the table with a quiet thud, she began to tease the condensation on the outside of the glass with her fingers. Her eyes remained focused on me, but her haphazard hand movements sliding along the glass told me she was nervous. "What are your parents like?"

I was slightly taken aback that she'd still be interested in a response regarding my mom and dad.

"They're awesome. My mom and dad have been married for nearly thirty years and are still totally in love with each other." My parents still kissed and held hands, but I didn't mention that part. "They're kind and supportive and provided us with a good balance of spoiling, discipline, love, and fostering our independence. We learned that hard work reaps benefits, and practice and patience yield results."

"They sound really nice. I bet you were a challenge to handle when you were growing up." Her flat tone didn't sit well with me.

"Why would you say that?" I was a good brother to Charlie—I took her coffee, for heaven's sake. I spent time with my family, held down a stable job, and had my own place. I thought I was a fairly responsible person. *So why would she think I was difficult?*

"You kind of have this bad-boy vibe about you." She was very matter of fact in her response, which I again found disconcerting.

"I do?" I didn't drive a motorcycle or have any tattoos, so I wasn't sure where she'd get that vibe from.

"If we're truly going to be friends, I think we need to be honest with each other."

I nodded in agreement. It wouldn't be good if I lied to her.

"I'd like to know what your intentions are with me, because you clearly don't need any more friends." Her eyes jumped around the table before she settled her blue gaze back on me.

"I intend to ask you to go out with me for ice cream after dinner. Just the two of us." I couldn't help but smirk at her absurd comment. Her serious, although mysterious, attitude needed to lighten up a bit.

"I'm not going to have sex with you, Cam." Her direct shot at my ego was the first time in my life that I'd found a woman telling me she would *not* have sex with me incredibly hot.

"Geez, Lex. Get your mind out of the gutter. Ice cream isn't code for sex. It really means ice cream. Or frozen yogurt, or a snow cone, or whatever you like." My remark was meant to be jovial, but I wasn't sure if she understood my attempt at humor.

A blank expression fell across her face. "I typically have a fairly good read on people, but, Cam, you surprise me." There was a dark truth beneath her confession, and it made me wonder what had happened to her that would've made her distrust people so much.

"Is it me, or just men in general?" I couldn't put my finger on her angst, but there was certainly suspicion, doubt, cynicism—something.

"This conversation has quickly gotten personal." She shifted her weight backward and leaned into her chair as she blew out a contemplative sigh. "I haven't had a lot of friends over the years. It's probably because I'm hesitant to share much of myself. I'm a private person—not secretive, just private. Really, I just don't like to share my crap with anyone. So when someone gets too close, I tend to put a wall up." Laying her hands crossed in her lap, almost giving herself a hug at the waist, she leaned toward me slightly. "I'm truly trying to change because I'm probably missing out on experiences due to that wall. But if I can be completely honest with you, I'm feeling a little uncomfortable with the topic, and I feel that wall going up again. I'm sorry."

Even though innocence usually radiated from her, a hidden darkness appeared with mentions of her past. I found myself worried, and the urge to be protective filled my core. I wanted to reach across the table for her hand, but she was squeezing herself into a hug. I had seen that self-comforting mannerism from her before and it tugged at my heart.

"Lex, you don't ever have to share anything with me that you don't want to. I assure you that I'm a good friend. I'll do anything in the world for my friends. I can keep a secret, but I also can give space. I'm always here when one of my friends needs someone to listen, to give advice, to not pass judgment, to be brutally honest, to provide an alibi, to keep silent company, to laugh, to cry, and to lift heavy objects."

My off-the-cuff proclamation caused the serious tone hanging in the room to evaporate without any intention on my part. I could tell the climate had changed because she laughed at the end of my speech. And it was a genuine laugh. It wasn't a soft giggle, but a loud, heartfelt laugh. It was my new favorite sound. "Lift heavy objects, really?"

"You know, like, when I help my friends move. I'm pretty strong." I flexed my biceps, and she shook her head with the remnants of soft laughter at my prepubescent sense of humor.

"Okay." Satisfaction pursed her lips, and her mood suddenly seemed buoyant. "I'll get ice cream with you after dinner."

The next day, I couldn't wait to call Charlie and tell her about Lex and me. She must've sensed me thinking about her, because she called first. That happened with us sometimes. Charlie said that she and Louis were finally going to make a go at a real relationship. It figured that once I began to have genuine feelings for a woman, my sister stole my thunder. Then again, maybe she couldn't give in to those emotions she had been feeling until I was able to. I'd heard that about twins. That if one felt something, the other would, too. For example, I could break my arm, and Charlie might feel the pain, even if she was miles away.

This was clearly a chicken and egg situation. It would be difficult to figure out the causation of which if this was a twin thing. *Was my ability to feel like I could become serious about a relationship the reason Charlie was able to? Or was Charlie finally admitting her feelings the reason that I was able to have those feelings at all?*

During our phone conversation, she'd invited me to go canoeing. Even though it was completely natural for my sister, Louis, and I to go on adventures together on the water, I assumed that since they were dating, I'd feel more like an outsider. I was sure to be the proverbial third wheel. But when she suggested I bring Lex along, I felt freed from the internal struggle. I was truly happy for Charlie and Louis, but the dynamics of our threesome had shifted. However, by bringing Lex into the mix, our weird threesome could transform into two couples. And that thought made me very happy.

5
ALEXIS

I was proud of myself for coming out of the shell that I had lived in for so long. I'd gone canoeing yesterday with Louis, Charlie, and Cam. Of course, Charlie and I had a lot in common, so for the first time in a very long time, I thought about letting my wall down. Those people made me feel like I could trust them. But most importantly, they didn't make me feel like an outsider. They accepted me. The three of them knew everything about each other. They'd been friends for ever, but they so openly welcomed me into their circle.

I used to always feel most comfortable spending time alone. I took refuge in my apartment or going for a long drive alone. But after spending time with these folks, I actually didn't find myself craving the alone time as much anymore. I'd begun to crave more time with them.

Even though it was obvious that Charlie and Louis were completely in love with one another, it wasn't awkward. I wasn't sure what had happened that caused them to take so long to get to where they are, but they were completely, utterly relaxed with each other.

We'd splashed each other during our time on the lake, and

I couldn't remember having a better time. I was just about completely soaked when we returned to shore, but I didn't care. They were genuine people. Superficial things seemed unimportant to them. We all got muddy and wet, but no one commented on how each of us looked. Their genuineness was so refreshing. There were no façades…no false qualities about any of them. I was starting to wonder when they would realize I was the one with the façade. I was the one pretending to be someone I wasn't. They had no idea who I was, where I had come from, or even what I'd done. I didn't want to lie, but I certainly didn't want them to find out the truth, either.

Cameron: Charlie and I go to the carnival every year. It's next weekend. You wanna go? Louis is coming also.

A carnival? I'd never been to one. I wasn't even sure what a carnival was. I knew there were rides, but I didn't have a clue about much else. I'd never actually been on a carnival ride before. I supposed that it could be fun.

Just as I began to tap a response to Cameron's text, there was a knock at my apartment door.

I peered out the peephole and saw him standing on the porch. With a swift pull, the metal door swung open. "You didn't even give me a chance to respond."

He pushed past me and entered my apartment without even asking if I was okay with him coming in.

I shut the door behind him while he glanced around my living room as if assessing my tastes or searching for some kind of answer. "I wanted to see where you live."

"Why?" I let out a forced huff and leaned my back against the cool door. *This is it. He is aware of something about my past. Don't jump to conclusions.* If he had uncovered something, I'd make him state what proof he claimed to have first before I tried to defend myself.

He turned around and looked at me suspiciously.

"Because we're friends, and it occurred to me that I don't even know where you live. We've been to breakfast. We've gone out to dinner. I bring you coffee at work, and we've gone canoeing on the lake, but I've never seen where you live, and you've never seen my place. Isn't it time we did that?" He drew his brows together, and for the first time since meeting him, I felt wary.

I wasn't sure what his motive was. So we shared a few meals, and I'd seen him at work a time or two…or twenty. Why did that mean he needed to see where I lived? I was new to having friends, so I'd admit, I wasn't sure what steps were involved with friendship. But I definitely didn't feel comfortable with him examining my place as if he were in search of incriminating evidence against me.

"I don't particularly enjoy unannounced guests."

His usually hard, chiseled features softened, and he held up his hands while taking a step away from me. "Are you okay?"

I guess I did kind of snap at him. And my voice may have sounded like gravel crunching beneath tires.

Seeing him scurry away left my emotions jumbled. I wasn't sure if I wanted him to stay or leave. I made sure to soften my voice before speaking again. "I just wasn't expecting anyone, and I really hate surprises." I honestly did. I tried my best every day to never be surprised about anything. I tried to anticipate every moment of the day.

"Okay. Sorry about that. Next time I will ask if it's okay if I stop by. I have a tendency to pop in on my friends on a whim. But I'll try to remember not to do that with you." He subtly dropped his hands to his sides and took a few steps toward me.

He shuffled in slow but purposeful steps, waiting for me to protest. Of course, I didn't. Rather than feel threatened by his closing proximity, I was intrigued. Once he reached the door that I still leaned against, he brought his face close to my own, and his warm breath tickled my lips. I stood motionless, watching the green outline of his hazel eyes dance with a hint of inquiry.

"If you want me to go, I will." His voice was husky yet soft. His presence was intoxicating, and I found it difficult to remain coherent while so close to him. I was glad I had leaned against the door, because I was pretty sure his swoony proximity could cause my already wobbly legs to give out. Then I would topple to the floor, and that would be really embarrassing.

"Cameron..."

"I told you, my friends call me Cam."

Heat flooded my senses, yet my skin prickled with goose-flesh. I hadn't realized at what point his hands came to rest against the door, but he had me caged in with each of his hands parallel to the sides of my face. *This is twice in the matter of two minutes this man has managed to sneak up on me.*

His lips curled upward into that devilish grin, revealing both a sweet and sexy appeal. I had never been so attracted to a man in my life—but he was attracted to *every* woman. Well, not *every* woman. He would never find me attractive. He preferred a woman with cute laughs and big boobs.

With that realization, I abruptly ducked beneath his braced arm and moved away from him in time to hear a throaty laugh. "Lex, I'm not going to bite you."

I realized our moment was over, but he took a step toward me as if attempting to get that moment back. I instinctively took a step backward, and his grin fell flat. His previously desired-filled eyes swirled with concern.

"Why are you so skittish?"

I continued my backward gait while he moved in my direction until I ran into the breakfast bar bordering my kitchen. The cool granite struck against my upper back. A worried expression came across Cameron's face as he heard the loud crack.

"Jesus, Lex. Did I do something to frighten you?"

I could tell he wanted to move toward me, but he resisted and remained planted several feet away.

I must've appeared like I was cowering from him. What he didn't realize was that I wasn't afraid of him. I was afraid of how I reacted when I was near him. People didn't scare me. This weakness I felt when he drew close was terrifying, though.

I fought to reassure him quickly. I didn't want him to feel like he had scared me. He'd wonder why and ask me questions I wasn't ready to answer. "I'm sorry. I just really don't like surprises."

His brows pinched together as he grabbed the back of his neck and blew out an exaggerated breath. "That's an understatement."

It was time to shake this whole ordeal off. So that's what I made up my mind to do. A subject change was definitely in order. "Do you feel like pizza?"

Cameron sent me a questioning look. "Pizza?" When I nodded, he added, "Yeah, I like pizza."

"I like Pizza Garden." I grabbed the menu attached to a magnetic clip on my refrigerator. "How about you?"

His dumbfounded expression indicated he was confused by my quick about-face. "That sounds…good?"

I understood that he was asking if I was good with what had just happened between us, and not whether the pizza was any good. But I didn't acknowledge his lingering question. I didn't really care if his inquiry was left dangling in the air between us, I would ignore it just the same.

"I like the veggie blast, but I bet you like the mighty meat." I took my cell from my pocket and began to dial, but Cameron grabbed the phone from my hand. I guess I should've anticipated that. This guy really distracted my focus.

"Are we going to just pretend like everything's fine and order pizza?" His hazel eyes begged me for answers, but he wouldn't get any.

"Is that okay?" If it wasn't, then I'd have to do something I really didn't want to do. I'd have to tell him to leave.

He drew in another deep breath. I may have overdone the pleading in my speech. "Okay. I didn't mean to surprise you. I won't let it happen again." Then, with that intense look he liked to shoot in my direction, he began speaking again. "Let's have the pizza delivered, and then we can talk about our carnival plans."

"I actually haven't been to a carnival before." I thought Cameron would choke on his pizza at my comment. I mean, I wouldn't actually let him choke. I'd been trained to do the Heimlich.

So here it comes. He'd realize I was weird and not want to be my friend anymore. "Well, it's never too late for your first time." *What?* He didn't ask why I'd never been as he sputtered his words amongst scattered coughs.

"I don't even know what really is even at a carnival, other than some rides."

He set his slice of pizza onto his paper plate, and again, I prepared myself for a judgmental response—or at least an uncomfortable question or two.

"You're going to love it." His eyes widened, and a smile stretched across his face. "There are a ton of games. I'm pretty good at them, so I could win you a prize." The confidence he had in his statement wasn't mistaken for arrogance.

"And the junk food is amazing. I *love* funnel cake, and caramel popcorn, and cotton candy."

I had never even heard what a funnel cake was, but it did sound delicious.

"Plus the soft pretzels, and nachos, and chili dogs."

"You eat all that junk in one night?" That was quite the menu he spewed out.

"Absolutely! And we ride the Ferris wheel, and Tilt-a-Whirl, and Merry Mixer, and Scrambler." Then he let out a small laugh. "Louis used to get really nauseous, so I'm not sure how much he'll eat before getting on the rides."

"It sounds like fun." It really did.

"I'm super excited to get to share your first time with you. I can't wait to see the look on your face when you experience it. I seriously look forward to sharing your enjoyment." This time, he didn't surprise me. I watched him reach across the table. I even let him brush his fingers across mine.

But what I didn't expect was that his touch would be so warm and comforting. I doubted that I'd ever had such a response to a simple touch before. He made me feel safe and, like, maybe I could trust him. That thought forced me to yank my hand away with more force than was necessary. This was crazy. I didn't trust men. I didn't think I trusted anyone, really.

Watching his empathetic expression and questioning eyes caused my heart rate to kick up its pace. Shortness of breath followed, and if I could hold off the hyperventilating, I'd keep myself from going into a full panic attack. *I don't do panic attacks,* I reminded myself. Well, at least I hadn't in a really long time.

"Lex, I'm not sure why I make you so uneasy, but I really like spending time with you. I promise that I'm a faithful friend. If there's *ever* something you want to tell me, I can keep a secret." He seemed genuine, and I really wanted to believe him. I had been carrying so many secrets for so long that I truly became quite exhausted with all the heavy burden.

"Cam, there's so much you don't know about me. And quite honestly, I'm really not ready to share. I didn't have a very good childhood, and I don't want to talk about it. I'm not saying I won't talk about it someday...I just don't want to right now." It actually felt pretty good admitting that much. "I've never been to a carnival, but I have seen the rides from the highway. When I was a kid, I wondered what it'd be like to go to one. Once I was old enough to go by myself, I realized I'd have to *go by myself.*" I extended my arm across the table and sought out his hand. "Thank you for offering to be the one to take me. I'm actually very excited about it." I probably sounded insincere, but I was very much looking forward to it.

I became more and more excited about the carnival as the week rolled by. I'd told myself numerous times over the years that I could do anything I wanted now that I was grown. But attending such a fair had been unattainable for so long that I thought I had lost interest in it until Cam asked. Now I couldn't wait.

I agreed to pick up Charlie and meet Cameron and Louis there. I was so excited that, by the time I arrived at her apartment, I could practically feel myself jumping up and down inside like a little kid on the way to see Santa Claus.

"Can we stop by the ATM on the way?" Charlie asked when she slid into the passenger seat. "The games require cash, and all I have is plastic."

"Sure. No problem." One stop along the way wouldn't

cause too much of a detour from the fun I was so looking forward to.

So I drove to her bank and parked in the lot while she walked up to the cash machine. I preferred the drive-up ATMs, but it was broad daylight, so I sat in the car with the engine running. I watched Charlie in my side mirror because you can't ever be too safe, right?

Because of my anticipation, I saw the large man before he even approached her. I turned off the engine and removed my key from the ignition, then I reached into my leather crossover bag. I felt the cool metal, and even though I hadn't touched it in forever, I felt the same comfort I always did with it in my hand.

As I emerged from my car, I memorized the features of the man that I perceived would try to hurt my friend. He was a white male with a large frame—probably six-foot-two and damn near a buck fifty—and shaggy blond hair. But when I caught his profile, I recognized him!

He grabbed ahold of Charlie from behind, and she squeaked out a cry.

"Hey, Otis!" Even though he currently had his large forearm around Charlie's neck, he stiffened at the sound of his name being called.

He slowly turned around, and with the safety already unlocked, I pressed the button to reveal the blade of the knife I carried with me. "Quicksilver," he mumbled. Good. He recognized me, too.

"That's right, Otis. You and I go way back." Most people would probably be scared in this situation, but I wasn't. Confidence and empowerment swirled within me. I always felt like I could take on the world with a knife in my hand, just like I did that night five years ago when I used a kitchen knife to defend my mother and me from her boyfriend. "Let... The... Girl... Go," I spat through clenched teeth.

"Not until she gives me her money." He was dead wrong if he thought, even for a second, that he'd get anything from either of us.

I stifled a laugh, which seemed to irritate him. Sheer panic shone in poor Charlie's eyes as she struggled to free herself from the grip Otis had around her neck. She kicked and tried to stomp on his feet, but he was solid and unmoving despite her efforts.

"Like I said, we have history with each other." My voice didn't hold any semblance of a quiver. "But now, you're too old to go back to juvie, and you don't want to go back to big-boy jail."

The whites of his eyes appeared to grow larger in the background of his light brown irises.

"Don't make the wrong choice here, Otis. I'm faster than you." I gritted my teeth and squinted before I forced out what needed to be said. "I'll catch you and won't hesitate to sink my knife into you. I will drive it in again and again and then watch your mangled body bleed to death. You remember what happened to Dragon, don't you?"

Charlie's rough gasps and coughs echoed louder as he squeezed tighter. He remained quiet, but the hatred in his expression toward me was evident. I didn't care that he was practically baring his teeth at me like a dog ready to attack, that his face was a dark shade of purple, or that the vein in his neck was visibly throbbing.

"But hey, you remember that I'm no snitch. So let her go, and I'll turn the other way. I won't call the cops, your case-worker, or your parole officer."

He continued to wear an intense, fevered stare, but when he finally huffed, he released Charlie from his grasp and shoved her away. The momentum had her stumbling forward while Otis scurried away, disappearing behind the building.

Charlie grabbed at her neck and took several quickened breaths.

"Get in the car."

She obeyed without reluctance while I folded up my blade and placed it back into my bag. Once safely back in the car with the doors locked and the windows rolled up, I used the talk-to-text feature on my phone to send a message to Cameron.

Alexis: Charlie isn't feeling well. I'm going to take her back home. Raincheck on the carnival.

We headed back to her apartment in silence. I was relieved. I didn't want to talk about it. I learned a long time ago that talking about stuff that happened on the streets was a good way to bring trouble. So I hoped she wouldn't want to say anything.

Charlie was still visibly shaken, so I walked with her up to her apartment. With trembling hands, she couldn't unlock her door. I was glad I'd made the decision to see her safely inside. She managed to shuffle her way to the couch and collapsed onto the cushions. *Should I stay and make sure she's okay, or should I go?* This was awkward.

I pulled over the barstool from her breakfast bar and perched myself on it. "Do you want me to get you some water?" I wasn't sure what to do when she shook her head. I sat in the same spot while Charlie remained face down on her couch for several moments.

As I was about to excuse myself, the doorknob jiggled, and the door of her apartment flew open with Cameron and Louis entering like a storm blowing through an unsuspecting town.

Louis plopped next to her on the couch and rubbed the back of her head. "Sweetheart, are you okay?" It must be nice to have someone care about you like that.

Suddenly, without warning, she began wailing pitiful

cries. She sat up and leaned into him before sobbing violently into his chest. I was sure the T-shirt he wore would soon be saturated with her unrelenting tears. Cameron glanced in my direction, but I quickly averted his gaze.

Louis held Charlie and murmured soothing words of comfort while rubbing her head as she continued to cry. I never saw Charlie upset about anything. I had worked alongside her for nearly a year. I had seen her take care of a dying child, massive stroke victims, and trauma patients with non-survivable injuries. She would never even bat an eye. She would take care of the patients the best she could and then move onto the next disaster without missing a beat. It was surreal to see someone who witnessed such tragic events be so shaken by a failed mugging.

Cameron approached me as I remained fixated on the puddle Charlie had created on her couch. Because I was usually aware of my surroundings, I was mindful he was right next to me before he spoke. "What the hell is wrong with her?"

I ignored him, but Charlie leaped out of Louis's grasp and briskly walked the two strides from the couch to where I was standing and threw her arms around me. I hated hugs. I mean, I *really* hated hugs. They were smothering and suffocating. Claustrophobia swept throughout my core when my space was violated. But for some reason, at that moment, I felt like she needed me to hug her back. She needed me to be like Louis. To hold her and let her know she was okay. So I lifted my arms from my sides and circled them around her. I patted her back and then pulled away. I wanted to comfort her, but there was definitely a time limit to an embrace.

"Thank you, Alexis." She looked up at me with tears still streaming down her red, puffy face. "I'll never be able to repay you."

Louis stood from the couch, and now I had three pairs of

eyes on me. I didn't get uncomfortable all that often, but at that moment, I felt like I wanted the floor to open up and swallow me into another place. I didn't really care where, just as long as it was anywhere other than right there, at that moment.

"Alexis said you weren't feeling well. What the hell happened?" Cameron swept his blazing stare from me and to his sister.

Charlie hiccupped a few quiet sobs and took a deep breath before speaking. "I got jumped at an ATM, and Alexis saved my life."

"Shit!" Louis grasped Charlie's face. I could tell he was in paramedic mode as he looked her up and down, assessing her for injuries. "Are you hurt?" His look of concern for her was definitely heartwarming. "I should take you to the ER, so you can get checked out."

"No!" Charlie pulled away from his grasp. "I'm *not* going to the ER. I'm fine." ER nurses *hate* to be patients at all. And none of us would willingly go to the ER as a patient. Since she was still conscious, I didn't think Louis would win this argument.

"Did you call the police?" Cameron asked with a hint of expectation in his tone.

Charlie's tear-filled gaze flew to me, and I gave her the "I don't want to talk about this anymore" face. I grabbed my car keys that I had tossed onto her end table when I entered her apartment. I was leaving—now.

I really could've been faster about my exit, but I guess my reflexes weren't as sharp as they used to be, because before I could turn the doorknob, Cameron's hand was on my upper arm. The warmth of his touch made me want to stay, so I released my fingers from their clutch on the doorknob.

"One of you had better start talking." I wasn't facing Cameron, but I recognized it wasn't his voice. It was Louis.

Cameron didn't release his grip on my arm, though. It was firm but not hurtful.

"A man grabbed me from behind at the ATM, Alexis pulled a knife on him, and he let me go." She made the incident sound very matter-of-fact and simple. I liked that about her. No need to embellish the situation. "I'm sorry, Alexis. I had to tell them. They're my family. And now, you are, too."

Then another squeezing sensation wrapped around me, taking my breath away. Cameron forcefully reeled me into him and encircled his strong arms around me while I still had my back to him. Again, I didn't feel smothered. I didn't even feel like I needed to break free. I could actually feel his gratitude as his chin rested on top of my head. His thankfulness seeped out as he hugged me. That warmth spread through me, and I didn't want it to end.

He spun me around after he released me from his warm embrace. Then his hazel eyes penetrated me to the point that, I swear, he could see right into my soul. "Is this true?"

I couldn't lie. Not when he maintained that penetrating gaze. So I reluctantly nodded in acknowledgment. I didn't expect what happened next. He kissed me. It was brief, but his lips connected with mine, and then another hug followed.

I felt woozy. Spots danced before my eyes as I let my torso melt in his strong arms. His body crushing against mine created a sensation within my belly that had never once happened in my whole twenty-one years alive. The wonderful phenomenon felt like the tickling of butterfly wings flapping against the walls of my insides. "Charlie's right," he said into my hair as he continued to hold me tight. "You are family now."

I laughed and broke away from his grasp. I was just getting used to these people being my friends. I certainly wouldn't take it as far as them being my family. Family sucked. I hated them. But I didn't hate these people.

Cameron must've sensed my displeasure, because he pulled me toward him again. He didn't push himself against me this time. He grabbed my hands and searched my face. Then a gratitude-filled smile deepened across his lips as those light brown eyes with their golden flecks cast at me. I really thought I could melt right there. His smile was genuine. I had seen him grin and smirk at the girls at work, but this was different. This was meant for me. It felt special. I couldn't even begin to describe how my senses exploded knowing that I did something to make him beam like that.

"When we were eight, the three of us went swimming in the lake." His lips flattened, and his megawatt grin faded with the change in his serious tone. "I was wearing water shoes, and when I jumped in, the elastic band on one of them got caught on a limb that was buried deep beneath the water's surface." He broke his gaze with me only long enough to glance at Louis and Charlie behind him. But his eyes found mine before he began speaking again. "I have no idea how long I was under, but Louis quickly became aware that something was wrong. He jumped in after me and freed my foot. Things afterward are a little hazy, but without being told by anyone, there's no question in my mind that he saved my life that day. He's been my brother ever since."

"How about just saying I'm family," Louis sputtered from over Cam's shoulder. "Because otherwise, it'd be weird that your brother is dating your sister."

"And you conveniently left out the part about how I had to help Louis drag your ass out of the lake and onto the shore." Charlie snickered through her muffled hiccups.

Charlie and Louis laughed. Even Cam let out a chuckle. I didn't, though. I was sure I stared at him with a blank expression. Because I had no idea what to say. I really wasn't sure even what to do. I just stood there, wilting with his hands still holding mine.

"You look overwhelmed. Are you okay?" He gave me a concerned look…I think. I wasn't sure if I'd ever had someone look at me with concern before. Again, I nodded. "We can't ever repay you, but is there anything at all we can do?"

"I just wanted to go to the carnival," I said meekly. I sounded pathetic. They all thought I had performed some amazing, life-saving act. I didn't feel like I had. I didn't expect repayment.

Cameron stifled a laugh. "Well, then. Okay. I'm taking you to the carnival."

I didn't mean that I *still* wanted to go to the carnival after what had happened, but Cameron insisted on taking me. He even offered to drive since Louis and Charlie decided to stay behind at her apartment and decompress. I hoped she was okay. I guess the incident really shook her up. I probably didn't even realize anymore that a normal person's reaction to that kind of incident would be terrifying. To me, it was just another day. I wondered what the likelihood would be that Cameron didn't bring it up for the rest of the evening. He was pretty quiet while driving his truck to the carnival grounds. *I needed to break the ice somehow.*

"I'm surprised your mother let you three go near water again after your near-drowning episode."

He let out a whooshed sigh of relief. He must've been waiting for me to be the first to speak since leaving his sister's apartment. "It's not like she could've stopped us. We weren't happy unless we had at least one foot in the water at all times." The irony wasn't lost on me, given his shoe was the reason for his near demise. "If we weren't in the water, on the water, or near the water, we'd go crazy. We'd swim, go canoeing, or fish all day, every day."

I pictured a young Cameron playing in the water. He obviously still loved being on the water from the fun we'd had the other day on the lake in a canoe. I doubt I would've enjoyed myself if I hadn't been with him. He just seemed to make everything better. Every experience, every smell, every taste, every place, everything was more exciting and intense with him. *Am I going crazy?* This wasn't me at all. I'd gotten pretty good at doing things by myself. I'd gone out to dinner, to the movies, grocery shopping, and to the beach by myself. However, going anywhere with Cameron—Cam—made me really happy. I must not have realized just how unhappy I was before. Being away from my parents and able to support myself had been my goal for so long, so I guess I just figured I'd be happy when I reached that goal.

Now I realized there was so much more to life than having a place to live and money to buy food and clothes. Sure, I took psychology in high school and college. I understood Maslow's theory of hierarchy of needs. It took me twenty-one years of life to have my physiological and safety needs met. Now I could move onto the part of the pyramid that included friends and intimate relationships. The first time I'd heard his theory and seen that damn pyramid, I remember thinking that Maslow was full of crap, but after understanding it, I realized he might've been onto something. If his theory had any actual truth to it, then I was onto the next step, which included *belonging* and *love*. Charlie, Cam, and Louis had all done their best to make me feel like I belonged. I felt very much part of their group, and I'd never felt part of a group before. Even at the hospital when we worked as a team to provide the best patient care, I just felt like I was doing a job rather than truly having a sense of belonging.

As I pondered a little more, I realized I'd never had the feeling to protect someone else from danger like I had today with Charlie. I was always so preoccupied with keeping myself safe, I probably never even noticed that someone else might need help more than I did. I was glad that I was able to help Charlie earlier. I wondered how long it would be before I was confronted about carrying a knife. Cam hadn't been very judgmental about me thus far, but I was sure that would all change at a moment's notice.

"You've been super quiet during this drive," Cam said while still firmly holding his gaze on the road ahead of him. "Are you sure you feel up to going to a carnival? It'll still be here tomorrow, if you would rather go then."

Feeling terrible, I felt my chest tighten and my spine curl forward. He was probably just as shaken as his sister was about what had happened earlier. "I should've never agreed to let you take me to the carnival after what happened to Charlie."

"Are you kidding? I'd take you anywhere you want to go right now." He snickered, causing me to arch my brow and straighten my posture. "You could ask me to take you to Mexico, and I'd start driving."

I smiled at his comment. He really was sweet. I prided myself on being a pretty good judge of character. I observed people closely, and they rarely surprised me, but Cam had the ability to throw me off-kilter. He'd been able to shock me on more than one occasion.

"Maybe you can take me to Mexico later." I playfully tossed a smile back at him. "You promised to win me a prize at the carnival, so I plan to hold you to that promise."

He reached across the seat and pulled at my hand. Rather than just brush the top as he'd done previously, he laced his fingers with mine, creating an incredibly intimate hold. "I always keep my promises."

I believed him. God help me, but I did. "You have been incredibly nice to me when you barely know anything about me, especially since I haven't exactly been very supportive of letting you get to know me with not wanting to talk about my past."

"You're not ready to tell me all about yourself yet." *How is it that he understands me so well?* "You said you had a crappy childhood, and that you didn't want to talk about it. One day you'll tell me. You just don't trust me yet."

I began to open my mouth to speak, but Cam shook his head. "It's okay. We're friends. When you want to confide in me, you will. I won't pry. It's not who I am. I'm supportive of my friends, and okay, maybe sometimes a little meddlesome, but Charlie and Louis deserved it."

"What are you rambling about?" I was happy he had deflected the subject away from me and to his sister and best friend instead.

"Five years ago, Louis told Charlie he was in love with her." He pulled into the fairground parking lot without ever letting go of my fingers. "Charlie told him she didn't love him back, so he ran away and just showed back up this summer." He parked the truck and once putting the vehicle into park, he turned and looked at me. "I should've chased after him, but I left the two of them alone to figure things out for themselves. After enough time passed, I figured they just weren't meant to be. However, after seeing the two of them together again, I wasn't able to idly stand by and watch them be miserable." He squeezed my hand. "When I see you nervous or unhappy, it breaks a little piece of my heart. Because I can't stand to see people I care about miserable."

"We just established that you barely know me. How can you say you care about me?" I rolled my eyes and pulled away from the intimate hand-holding gesture.

He switched off the ignition and removed his keys, but

then returned his attention to me. "I'm not sure why you find that so hard to believe. You saved my sister's life. But even before tonight, I have enjoyed spending time with you, and I consider you a friend. So of course I care about you." His eyes narrowed in annoyance. And once again, I felt terrible about causing him unsettled feelings.

I swallowed hard and felt a sniffle beginning to surface. The kind of sniffle that might be followed by tears. "Cam." I blew out a long breath. "I haven't had a real friend in a very long time, so I may need a little bit of an adjustment period. Additionally, I haven't dated in quite a while, and I've never had a boyfriend before, so I may be a little awkward around you. Just realize it isn't anything you've done. It's my lack of experience. I am really unsure how to act around most people."

6
CAMERON

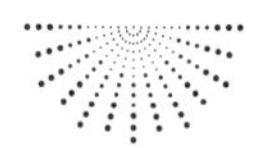

Charlie had mentioned that Alexis was inexperienced. I just assumed she meant regarding sex. I had no idea the magnitude of her inexperience. I told her I was okay with waiting until she was ready to confide in me, but I was becoming more than a little curious about why she hadn't had friends in a while or ever had a boyfriend. *Never having been in a canoe or never going to a carnival may be normal, right? And what's the deal with carrying a knife? If she's so inexperienced, how can she be such a badass?*

Maybe she didn't trust me with the secrets of her past, but she had trusted me with some of her new adventures. I hoped some new opportunities would make good memories for her. So I would focus my attention on that. She'd turned my insides two times to Tuesday, and I couldn't remember ever feeling so captivated by a girl. I wanted to be with her for all her firsts. She fascinated me for sure, just like Charlie had pointed out. Damn, I hated when she was right.

"You don't ever have to *act* around me. I like you just the way you are." I leaned into her and gave her one quick peck on her cheek before opening my truck door and making the long walk to the carnival entrance.

Normally, after spending this much time with a woman, I would've slept with her by now. And very possibly moved on to another one. But I had no desire to slam forward at lightning speed with Lex. I wanted to savor every single moment with her. I wasn't kidding when I said I wanted to be there for all her firsts. I truly did.

I loved seeing Lex's face when she tried funnel cake. The swirly ribbon of pastry covered in powdered sugar may be strange-looking fried dough, but the taste created an explosion in your mouth. And as I had already planned, we ate chili dogs and cotton candy and nachos and soft pretzels. We shared, but she definitely held her own with the buffet of junk food.

The Tilt-a-Whirl and the Scrambler didn't make her lose any of the crap she'd digested, so I considered it a win in my eyes. A woman with a cast-iron stomach was totally a turn-on. After holding her hand in my truck, I wanted to reach for her hand several times throughout the evening, but I'd restrained myself somehow.

She had never been on a Ferris wheel, so I left that ride to be the culmination of our evening. I was excited to show her the view from the top. The expansive sight spread across town and all the way to the coastline, where the ocean could be seen meeting the sky at the horizon. I'd seen it many times before, but I couldn't wait to see her reaction to it.

We played several games, and I won her a large stuffed teddy bear at the ring toss booth. She actually jumped up and down and clapped her hands when I won. And that smile across her face when I let her pick out the prize was a memory I would cherish for a long time. I'd been to the carnival more times than I could count, and although my sister and I always had a wonderful time, nothing could compare to watching the experience through the eyes of someone seeing the carnival for that initial time.

"Are you nervous about being up so high?" I asked Lex while we waited in the line for the Ferris wheel.

She clutched the stuffed animal against her chest and retained that elated smile. "I'm not afraid of heights." She laughed sweetly. And oh, how sweet she sounded.

"I don't imagine you're afraid of anything. You're probably fearless." She shrugged without commitment.

"Right now, I'm honestly too happy to be afraid of anything." She reached out and grabbed my hand. I suddenly felt like I was fourteen again.

Nervousness prickled my skin, and my hand started to perspire within her grasp.

"I can't thank you enough for sharing this evening with me." Her smoky blue eyes swirled with appreciation.

"Thank you for letting me be the one you shared this new experience with." I couldn't go without touching her or holding her for a moment longer, so I pulled her toward me. She was still clutching that damn bear, so I crushed her arm and that bear against my chest as I embraced her.

I felt her relax beneath my embrace, and she actually snuggled in closer to my chest. I hadn't expected that. She'd always seemed to have a firm distance in place when it came to me, like she needed a buffer for her personal space. Maybe that was one barrier she'd allowed to come down.

I drove Lex back to Charlie's apartment complex, where her car was still parked from earlier in the day. I pulled into the parking spot next to hers.

"So maybe I'll see you sometime this week?" I didn't want the evening to end, but I wasn't about to try and press my luck.

"You mean for coffee delivery?" That adorable smile swept across her face again, brightening her blue eyes between her long eyelashes.

"Of course, but maybe another time, too?" I turned toward her and felt myself become nervous again. "I can invite Charlie and Louis if that makes you feel more comfortable."

"I would love to spend time with you again. Just text me what the plans are, and I'll be there." She broke our gaze and dug into the contents of the bag draped across her torso to find her keys. As she began to push the passenger side door open, I saw a familiar symbol dangle from her keyring.

I grabbed her hand before she could exit my truck. "You have a Batman keychain?"

"Yeah, I do." There was a pensive shadow in her eyes as her shyness returned when she tried to explain. "Do you think that makes me weird?"

I dropped her hand before my own explanation. "Are you kidding? I have all seven movies on DVD. I love them all, but Michael Keaton is still my favorite Batman."

She liked Batman. Perhaps I could fall in love after all.

"Perhaps I can come by sometime and watch a movie? I haven't seen them all." She wore an expectant look on her face, waiting for my answer.

Perhaps she could come by? She could come by anytime. "It's still early. Do you want to watch a movie now?" *Please say yes.*

"Maybe some other time, Cam. I know what the time says, but I'm exhausted. I really just want to head back to my place and relax." She brushed against my hand again with her soft, delicate palm. "I really had a great time with you this evening. Thanks for that." And just like that, she withdrew from my hand and shifted out of her seat and out the door.

I watched as she safely pulled out of the parking lot, and then I retreated out of my truck and to my sister's apartment. I knocked loudly on her door. I had a key, but now that she was dating Louis, I always knocked. I really wasn't interested in barging in on a make-out session between the two of them.

"Your night ended early," Charlie said in a voice heavy with sarcasm as she stood within the open doorway. "Everything all right?"

I pushed past her and collapsed onto her sofa with a loud swoosh. Then, covering my face with my hands, I let out a loud, exaggerated sigh. Footsteps approached me, and they weren't the light steps of a female. They were heavy. I parted my fingers and peered through them. Louis loomed over me, studying my face.

I quickly pulled my hands off my face and sat up. "What the hell are you looking at?" I scoffed at the man I still considered a brother.

"I was making sure you weren't sick."

Using both hands, I shoved him away. He was only slightly knocked off balance, but he did take a step back while he snickered at me.

"He's *love*sick." And then my sister made an annoying, lip-smacking, smooching noise numerous times while puckering her lips.

I picked up a throw pillow from her couch and launched it at her. Because there wasn't much weight to the pillow, she had plenty of time to dodge it before she and Louis both fell into a fit of laughter.

I stood up from the couch. If I was going to have these

two poke fun at me, they were going to have to do it with me looming over them. "What the hell is so damn funny?"

Charlie was the first to take some deep breaths and try to calm herself out of the side-splitting hysterics she had been immersed in. "It's eight thirty at night, and Cam Callahan is at his sister's apartment, rather than spending the night with his date for the evening."

"What happened? Did she turn you down?" Louis was quick to display a sarcastic frown while trying to hold back his amusement.

"I didn't get turned down," I retorted, trying to hide my humility. "I wanted to make sure Lean Bean was okay."

"That's bullshit, Cameron." Charlie went back and forth between calling me Cam and Cameron. She doesn't call me by my full name for any particular reason, like, for say, when she wanted to express her displeasure about something or have me appreciate the severity of a situation. She wasn't happy that I was lying to her though. We were best friends. Even though she wasn't always sure what I was thinking, she could always tell when I wasn't truthful. Damn the twin connection.

"I *do* want to make sure that you were okay, but I also have confidence that you're under Louis's protection." I could feel my stature relax.

"You didn't do anything to Alexis that I'll have to apologize to her for, did you?" Charlie's arched brow rose in question.

"I didn't do anything to embarrass you, I swear." I held up my hands in surrender.

"So what the hell happened?" Louis inquired. He was never this interested in my exchanges with a woman before.

I fell back into the cushions of the couch again. "I asked her to come to my place and watch a movie, and she basically said she would rather be alone than spend any more time with me tonight."

"Really? That's what bruised your ego?" Charlie swatted my legs, giving me the sign to move over and accommodate her to sit alongside me. Once I shifted a little to the right, she squeezed in next to me. "She spent the last several hours with you, didn't she?"

"Maybe she'd be more comfortable if she had more time in a group setting versus one on one with you." *When did Louis get all girly?*

"Louis is right. Maybe the four of us could do something together?"

I would let Charlie think she initiated that suggestion so I didn't have to admit that I'd already mentioned that scenario to Lex.

"Good idea. How about roller skating?" The cringing shudder I received from them both was the reaction I expected. I was fully aware that would strike a nerve with them. I mean, what kind of friend would I be if I didn't razz the people I cared about a little?

"Man. That was low. You were there when I broke my arm the last time I went roller skating." Louis shook his head and rubbed his right arm up and down in response to the memory. It'd happened years ago, but you would've thought by his reaction that it had happened last week.

I laughed under my breath at the satisfaction I had earned.

"Poor Louis." Charlie stood up and took over rubbing his arm. *Ick!* "It was the day before our last day of school, and we went on that class field trip to the skating rink."

The three of us were silent briefly as we recalled the events leading up to his orthopedic injury.

I wasn't going to let my sister beat me around the rink again. It was bad enough I got shown up by my best friend, but

I certainly wasn't going to let Charlie win the race around the loop.

I pushed other children out of the way so I could catch up to her. She, of course, heard me approach, so she did her best to propel herself forward as fast as she could. I was about to close in on her, though...until Louis decided to pull himself out of the race and help Lean Bean beat me! At first, he pulled her behind him. Then he used his own momentum to push her forward. She whizzed past me, and I struggled to maintain my lead. I began falling behind.

Louis began to roll his way across the diameter of the rink to help her gain momentum again instead of sticking to the outside perimeter. No way, buddy! I'm winning this race. *As he approached us, I shoved him with all my force. His forward momentum being struck by an opposing force, not only caused him whiplash, but it also caused him to lose his balance. He used his outstretched hand to brace his fall, and then we all heard it. The thunderous clap of the wrist bones being cracked.*

At first, I continued skating; I thought he fell but was okay. I only meant to stop him from helping Lean Bean win the race. I didn't mean to hurt my friend. Being the kinder heart of our twinship, Charlie went to Louis first. He began to cry. Geez. I made my best friend cry.

I skated over and helped him to his feet. The scowl that my twin threw at me nearly knocked me off my feet as well. She was furious. I'd never *seen her this angry with me. I felt awful for what had happened, and I hoped they would forgive me. I never wanted to compete with these two again. I cared more about them than anyone else in the world...well, except maybe my mom and my dad.*

"I swore that day that I would never compete with you two over anything ever again." We couldn't help ourselves. The three of us erupted into unrelenting laughter.

We tried to catch our breaths and stifle our snorting

cackling, but it was extremely difficult. Even thinking there was a time when we wouldn't have competed against each other was complete absurdity.

"Well, that was probably fifteen years ago," Louis said, trying to regain his composure.

"Yes. It was second grade." Charlie reclaimed her seat next to me. This time, Louis wedged himself onto the couch as well so that we were both on either side of my sister. "Then, on the last day of school, you wouldn't even let me sit next to you on the school bus home. Louis got to stay home that day, and you chose to sit next to that girl instead of me." She poked her index finger into my chest. "What was that name you called her?"

"Butterfly."

"Holy crap. I forgot about her. She used to cry every day on the bus. Cam was her knight in shining armor." Louis clutched his right hand over his heart and then draped his left hand across his forehead in a dramatic swooning effect.

Sniggering bubbled beneath Charlie's breath again. "Dark Knight, maybe. She used to call him Batman, remember?"

Louis and Charlie chuckled at the memory. I was not amused. I did not find that memory humorous at all. That was the last day I saw the Butterfly girl.

"Why can't I sit next to you today? After all, you're the reason Louis isn't here to ride home with me." Charlie stomped her foot in the aisle of our school bus.

"Because I always ride home next to Butterfly. I'm saving the seat next to me for her." I loved my sister, but I rode with her this morning. I had to be available for Butterfly after school. Not to mention, I'd be with Charlie all summer. Today would be the last day I'd see Butterfly until school started again in September.

"Sometimes I hate you." She stuck out her tongue and then

relented to the seat across from me, next to Tommy-still-sucks-his-thumb.

I snarfed a laugh and briefly put my thumb in my mouth, assuring her that I was aware what she had to deal with sitting next to Tommy. She rolled her eyes at my gesture.

Butterfly waved to me while walking up the steps into the bus. She had a smile on her face when she saw me, but it quickly faded as she came closer. I slid in toward the window to allow her room to sit next to me. I pulled out my lunch box like I had done every day for the entire year, grabbed the mini Kit Kat bar, and handed it to her. My mom had agreed to keep Kit Kats in the house if I kept my grades up.

Needless to say, I'd received straight As on every report card I had brought home this year. So I always had a Kit Kat in my lunch. Charlie got Little Debbie snacks, and Claudette preferred Doritos. We were all good students, so I assumed Mom continued to indulge us with the junk food incentives in the hopes we would continue to do well in school.

Butterfly reached for the Kit Kat, and although her lips were turned upward in a smile, she had tears streaming down her face. I had hoped all year for just one day where she wouldn't cry. "I'm going to miss you this summer, Batman."

"Nah, you're just going to miss the chocolate."

She giggled and wiped the tears from her face with her fingers.

"We'll see each other again soon, though."

"What if we don't ride the same bus next year?" Her look of concern made me sad.

"Then I'll find you. I'll keep looking for you until I find you." And then I hugged her because that always helped my sisters feel better when they were sad.

But she didn't like my hug. She pushed me away. "How would you be able to find me? You are just a little kid like me."

I was still shocked at the way she shoved me off her, but I managed to confidently say, "Because I'm Batman."

"I wonder whatever happened to her," Charlie said, snapping me out of the pull from my distant memory.

"Maybe she moved away," Louis offered. They both shrugged.

"So how about a pizza night soon?" I suggested in an attempt to change the subject. They both looked at me with questioning eyes. "So I could invite Lex over. She likes delivery from Pizza Garden. Maybe we could watch a movie?"

"I've never seen you so obsessed over a girl before." A teasing smile tugged at the corners of Charlie's mouth.

I would just have to break down and tell her. I told her everything, so this wouldn't be any different. "You were right, Lean Bean. I'm fascinated by her. I like being around her. I admire and respect her, and I get so excited when I get to see her." I ignored Louis, who made a gagging noise next to Charlie while sticking his finger into his open mouth.

"Wow. I'm not sure whether to be impressed that you used so many adjectives to describe a girl, or that your description spells out FLARE." She must have seen the look of confusion I felt across my face because she began to provide an explanation. "Fascinated, like, admire, respect, and excited…they create the acronym, FLARE."

I wasn't sure whether to be shocked that she paid that much attention to what I had said, or that she could think of acronyms that quickly.

"You mean, FLARE, like that emergency firestick that we lay on the shoulder of the road at a traffic accident scene?" I could count on Louis, who was also a paramedic, to take the conversation in another direction. I appreciated that from him.

"Yes! That's it!" My sister's eyes widened and brightened

as if she just had a lightbulb moment. "Alexis is your emergency firestick. She gets you all hot and bothered."

Louis bounced a look back and forth between Charlie and me, waiting for one of us to speak. But we were very good at the quiet game. Neither one of us would be the first to say anything. We could be incredibly stubborn. Several moments ticked by without any words exchanged between the three of us as we sat on the couch. We sat staring at each other in silence and awkwardness for probably fifteen or twenty minutes.

"So when should we have pizza?" Louis sucked at this game. While he was away for five years, Charlie and I had perfected this game. One of us would always cave. Because, like I'd mentioned before, we were best friends. Pretty soon, we would *have* to speak to each other. I would need to talk with her, or she would need to talk to me. I knew it was childish, but the first to speak had to take the other out for a Diet Coke.

"I'm thinking maybe Friday night?" Poor Louis. He was trying to get us to engage, but neither of us would budge. So I guess he did what he thought he needed to do. He crashed on top of both of us on the couch and began tickling us.

I never realized how strong he was before now. He had both Charlie and me pinned to the cushions while he tickled us senselessly. "Say stop at the same time on my count, and I will." He continued to poke at us. We were both laughing uncontrollably. "One...two...three."

"Stop!" we said in unison. He rolled off us and allowed us to peel ourselves out of the sinkhole of pillows.

Charlie slapped his shoulder. It was a move she'd often made when we were kids. "That wasn't nice, Louis." He loudly kissed her pouting lips. *Gross!*

"Okay, so that was a little nice." She leaned toward him

and started kissing him. I swear I saw her shove her tongue into his mouth before I had to look away.

"Jesus, you two!" I called, facing my back to them. "So pizza at my place on Friday night at seven." I hurriedly walked to the door without looking back in their direction. "Don't worry, I'll let myself out."

I continued out the door and kept walking toward the parking lot. When I reached my truck, I took my phone out and began to send a text once I was seated in the cab.

Cameron: Louis and Charlie are coming over to my place on Friday at 7pm for pizza and a movie. *Please* don't make me be alone with them! Say you'll come too.

Alexis: I'll think about it.

Cameron: You don't understand! They started making out right in front of me just a minute ago. [puking face]

Alexis: LOL [laughing smiley face]

Cameron: So please! Pretty please say you'll come over.

Alexis: Okay. Send me your address.

I watched the bubbles dance across my screen as she typed more.

Alexis: And maybe I'll talk with Charlie about the PDA [laughing smiley face]

Cameron: [smiley face] [smiley face] [smiley face]

Alexis: Maybe we can watch the Michael Keaton Batman? Since it's your favorite.

Cameron: [smiley face] [smiley face] [smiley face]

Now that I was back at the high school for work, weekends were the best for me to spend time with my friends. Lex and Charlie both worked on Tuesday night, so luckily, I didn't have to go six days without getting to see Lex again. I brought them coffee that night. As always, I also brought some for the other two ER nurses—Tiffany and Cecilia. I tried to be my friendly self, but I had zero desire to spend the few minutes I had flirting with the two of them. I spent every bit of my ten minutes with Lex. I said hi to my sister and the others. I wasn't rude by any means, but I was pretty sure I made it clear that I wasn't interested in anyone but Lex.

My nonchalant attitude toward Tiffany and Cecilia definitely hadn't gone unnoticed. Charlie had texted me Wednesday afternoon to tell me they were both heartbroken because it was obvious I had decided which ER nurse was my favorite.

My sister also teased me that she was disappointed that *she* wasn't my favorite. During our texting conversation, she also agreed to keep the PDA to a minimum. Maybe Lex had said something to her? Regardless, I hoped she held true to that. Don't get me wrong. I was super happy my two best friends were in a relationship together. It was probably always destined to be that way. Maybe they'd get married someday, and Louis would *really* become my brother like I'd wanted so desperately when we were kids. I wasn't like other brotherless boys. I didn't just want a brother. I specifically wanted *Louis* to be my brother.

Regardless that I completely supported their relationship, I was still getting used to the idea that they were intimate. I was aware they had sex. Charlie had told me all about their first time. She needed to talk to her best friend, so I stayed as objective as I could. But deep down, my stomach was tied in knots that the two of them had done that. Even with her telling me about that, it wasn't as bad as seeing them lust over each other with my own eyes. It made me extremely uncomfortable. But being friends with them for as long as I had, if I'd let on that the PDA bothered me, they would go into overdrive with the kissing and snuggling just to get under my skin. We liked to tease each other at every opportunity we got.

On Friday, Lex arrived at my apartment at seven o'clock on the dot. The food was delivered five minutes later, and at almost a quarter past, my besties finally showed up. I didn't want to imagine what they might've been doing that made them late. Louis had never arrived late to pizza night at the Callahan household when we were kids. It was every Friday, and much like tonight, we would eat while watching a movie. Of course, we lived with our parents back then, so it was in the basement of my childhood home instead of my own apartment. But compared to this day, Fridays, pepperoni, cheese, and movies…they still held similarities.

Charlie threw a package on my counter once she and Louis entered my kitchen. The red plastic covering told me what was in it, so I made up my mind to forgive her tardiness rather quickly.

"What'd you bring?" Lex asked.

"It's dessert." She held up the bag for Alexis to see. "Kit Kats, to be exact. Cam very rarely eats them, but they're his favorite."

"That's funny because they're my favorite candy bars, too." She glanced at the unopened plastic bag. "Some girls eat ice cream, but I always found refuge in the empty calories of a Kit Kat bar when depressed or faced with a dilemma."

"They say diamonds are a girl's best friend, but I'd argue that chocolate is." Both girls laughed in agreement and moved toward the stacked pizza cartons sitting on my kitchen table.

"I figured we'd eat in front of the TV so we can start the movie," I suggested as I grabbed a stack of plates from my cabinet.

"What are we watching anyway?" Louis tried to act interested, but I already knew he cared more about the free food and making out with my sister in the dark than what would actually be playing on my television.

"Batman," I said plainly. When I looked at Lex, I could see her lips curve into the faintest grin. Lex and I sat on the couch next to each other with food in hand.

"Ugh," my sister whined. "Michael Keaton?" Charlie dropped a cheesy slice onto a plate and walked toward the adjacent love seat. "Alexis, he made me and Louis watch that movie at least a dozen times the summer he bought the DVD."

"Well, it's my place, and it's my favorite." I stuck out my tongue at her like we used to when we were kids.

"Real mature, Cam. I get that the Dark Knight series isn't your favorite, but can't we still change it up? What's wrong with Val Kilmer or George Clooney?"

Louis plopped down next to Charlie on the love seat. "So, I'm thinking about getting a tattoo." That was a random comment from my best friend. He always had an idea how to distract my sister when he felt a disagreement developing between the two of us.

"We could get matching ones," she responded with a sarcastic grin. I could tell she was kidding.

"What would you get, Lean Bean?" I was totally going to feed into her comment, because I was fully aware that she was terrified of needles. It was ironic, considering she was a nurse. She claimed giving needles didn't bother her but receiving them did.

"I'm not sure." She rubbed her finger across her chin as if she was contemplating. "How about you, Alexis? If you were to get a tattoo, what would you get?" *Deflection. Nice tactic, Lean Bean. But completely unoriginal.*

"I already have one," Lex stated plainly between bites. Even though she responded nonchalantly, she found herself with three sets of eyes on her anyway. Having a tattoo seemed entirely unlike her, but then again, as she had pointed out, how much did I really know about her anyway?

"What is it?" Charlie's voice was laced with curiosity.

"*Where* is it?" Louis asked because, of course, location was his primary interest.

"It's a butterfly." Her gaze didn't waver from her cheesy, vegetable-laden slice of pizza. "On my bikini line."

Thank goodness she didn't see my reaction. I swallowed hard. Because I pictured a tattoo on her bikini line...a tattoo of a butterfly.

An overwhelming sense of shock flew through me. Wave after wave of astonishment came over me, causing my stomach to churn. My breath caught in my throat, and I could feel my pulse quicken. I had swallow hard to push the choking sensation back down. My heart quivered and twisted within my chest as the reality of the situation slammed into me. And that damn knot in my gut was begging to be released.

The nagging in the back of my mind refused to be silenced so I could gather my thoughts. The Batman keychain. The Kit Kats. The butterfly. The magnetic pull she had over me. The reason I felt the need to be with her. The explanation for the sudden wave of memories of second grade.

I shook my head, fully aware of what I had to do. So I abruptly stood and set my plate on the coffee table with a loud thud before prying Charlie's and Louis's from their grasps.

"Cam, what the hell are you doing?" Charlie mumbled around the food in her mouth. She made a futile attempt to retrieve her dish from my hold, but I moved it out of her reach.

"It's time for you and Louis to leave." I tried to send her a pleading look without Louis and Lex realizing what I was trying to do. I turned away from them and tossed the rest of their food into a carton. Then, as Louis approached me in the kitchen, I shoved the cardboard container into his abdomen. "Here, take some pizza to go."

I mouthed the word *butterfly* to my sister, and her lips curled up at the corners as her smile broadened with approval. She embraced me in a hug, and with a quick release, she grabbed my arm and glared her gray eyes directly at me. "You better text or call me...no matter what time it is."

I merely nodded. Louis appeared puzzled as he rubbed his chin and grimaced, but then again, he didn't observe the lip reading my sister had to decipher. While Louis was literally left holding the box, Charlie returned to a very confused Lex still sitting on the couch. "Louis and I have to go, but I'll see you soon." She leaned over to embrace Lex in a brief hug, nearly knocking the food off her plate.

"Maybe I should go, too." Lex tried to stand, but Charlie gently pushed her back into the cushions of the couch. She almost dropped her dish again. I wondered how difficult it would be to get hot cheese off the upholstery, since the event was more than likely to happen with the rate things were progressing.

I shot Charlie a "you've outstayed your welcome" warning and motioned her toward my door. Thankfully, she took the not-so-subtle hint I'd thrown at her. "Come on, Louis. Let's go eat at my place and watch Netflix."

They left, and since I was standing in my living room and Lex was sitting, I began to advance toward the couch. But I was hit with a thought before I completed the two strides.

"I want to show you something, but I have to get it." I pointed to the back of my apartment. "It's in my bedroom. Promise me you'll wait right here." I didn't wait for her response. All tension left my body and happiness took up residence in me as I literally skipped to my bedroom.

7
ALEXIS

I wasn't sure if I should stay or not. Cam was acting strange. Then again, Charlie was a little odd right before she left, too. Louis looked just as confused as I felt right now, so maybe it was a weird twin thing. I became more uncomfortable as the moments dragged by. I hadn't attempted to eat another bite of my pizza, so I decided to set it on the coffee table alongside Cam's abandoned slice.

A rustling noise came from a room at the end of the hallway when I stood. I didn't know what was going on, and I really began to feel uneasy. As if sensing my thoughts of abandonment, Cam emerged from the open door, which I assumed was his bedroom. He launched into a jog toward me, clutching a large sketchpad to his chest. Then, with a look of what appeared to be panic, he stood in front of me.

"You asked me once if I had ever been in love. And I'm very, very sorry because I wasn't truthful with my response." He pointed toward the couch, indicating he wanted me to sit. I complied with his unspoken request, and he continued to hold the sketchpad and sat not just next to me, but painfully close to me. His knees touched my own. "Please look at me, Lex."

I hadn't realized I wasn't looking in his direction. I was uncomfortable, and when I'd be uncomfortable, I zoned out. It was a defense mechanism I had developed long ago. When I didn't like what was going on around me, I would transport my mind to another place. Cam appeared nervous and anxious. His face was flushed, and his muscles were coiled. It was not his normal demeanor at all.

Once again, I conformed to what he asked of me and looked into his hazel eyes. He flipped open the spiral-bound pad with shaky hands and turned the picture to show me the sketched image. It was a beautiful drawing of a butterfly with yellow and orange hues and black outlining its wings. "I fell in love with a girl named Butterfly a long time ago." He searched my eyes for a sign that I might discern what he was referring to, but I didn't concede. "I couldn't get her out of my mind for years and years, so I began drawing butterflies."

I watched the sweat beading on his forehead for a moment before I found the courage to add my own confession. "I have to show you something too, but I don't want you to get all weird. Okay?"

Cam nodded, but still had apprehension hanging across his face. I pushed myself up from the couch and stood facing him. Then I pushed my shorts and panties down slightly over my hip to expose the tattoo I had inked along the left side of my bikini line. Cam's mouth dropped open as he reached toward me and touched the permanent picture with his index finger.

"It's the same butterfly I drew." He was right. It was the same colors, the same profile, the same details.

I snapped my clothes back into place, and Cam's finger relented. He dragged himself up slowly from the couch until his towering frame stood next to me. He didn't embrace me as I feared he might, which allowed me the opportunity to turn away from him. A new and unexpected warmth surged through me, mixed with a tumble of confusion. I didn't want him to witness those tormenting emotions bubbling to the surface and threatening to erupt. My mind was spinning, and I was desperately trying to conceal the inner turmoil.

I didn't want to croak words out, so I tried to calm myself before speaking. "I couldn't get you out of my mind, either. You told me you would find me. I kept hoping you would, but Batman never came back into my life." I totally croaked... like a whimpering frog.

A tense silence enveloped the room as he stepped toward me. I still had my back to him, but I could sense he was at a loss for words. He reached for my hand, but instead of grabbing my palm in his, or intertwining our fingers, he linked our thumbs together and stretched his fingers out like a wing. I felt myself surrender. I stretched my fingers out also and moved them in unison with his.

"I found you now, Butterfly." He brushed his face against my hair, and I felt the tension between us beginning to melt with his huskily whispered words. He stood tall behind me, but he leaned down, and I could feel his heated breath against the back of my neck. "I'm so, so sorry it took me this long." He unhooked his thumb from mine and applied light pressure with his hands to my upper arms so that I would turn to face him. His eyes were like embers burning in a fire that I thought had died out a long time ago. I wasn't sure how I didn't recognize those eyes until now. "I told you that we would be best friends, and I let you down. I promise that I will *never* let you down again."

"Butterfly and Batman. Best friends?" The tears filling my eyes stung, and I couldn't prevent them from spilling over soon. With my impending emotional breakdown, Cam released his grip on my arms and walked past me to his kitchen counter, where he retrieved the bag his sister had left behind and quickly returned to my side.

"These used to make you feel better." He ripped open the plastic bag holding the mini chocolate bars and offered me a Kit Kat.

I released a laugh just as a tear slipped from my eye. I snatched the chocolate candy from his hand, and a smile stretched wide across his face. I felt lighter somehow, but so exhausted all the same.

"Come on, Butterfly." He walked the two steps toward his couch and motioned me to follow him. "Let's finish our pizza and watch Batman."

In dazed exasperation, I stood frozen in my spot. I tried to force my confused emotions into order, but I couldn't figure out what to say or what to do. I felt like I couldn't even think straight as my brain continued its tumult. So I took a very long, cleansing breath like I had taught myself to do a long time ago when I felt overwhelmed. I truly was overwhelmed.

"Cam, I'm exhausted. I really just want to curl up in my bed right now. This whole thing"—I pointed between the two of us—"has been very emotional, and I really need a minute to myself to process it all."

Disappointment was written across his beautifully chiseled face. Why I hadn't recognized him until now seemed absurd. Of course he was my Batman; it was clear as day. "I just found you again, Butterfly." He reached for my hand, but I pulled away. "Please don't leave." Those damn hazel eyes and his murmured pleas killed me.

"I'm leaving for now, but we'll see each other again soon." I offered him a faint smile. Hopefully, he wouldn't try to stop me from walking out of his apartment. I really wanted to be by myself right now. I was on the verge of falling apart, and I didn't want him to bear witness to that. It had been a very long time since I'd let myself get so emotional that I could even allow myself to feel anything. Now I couldn't seem to avoid it. I needed to go before I lost all control.

I turned to walk away as his silky, throaty voice caressed me. "Lex."

I didn't turn around this time. I reached for the doorknob and felt it turn between my fingers.

"Please." The desperation and pleading in his voice were too much. I had to get the hell out of there.

The sound of a fist pounding into flesh woke me up again. Or maybe it was the woman's screams. I flipped over onto my abdomen and grabbed the pillow to pull over my head. Then I squeezed the stuffing over my ears and held tightly, hoping to drown out the sound. It was bad enough that I was aware of the hitting, but I *hated* actually hearing it.

My pillow did nothing to drown out my mother's cries, and I was tired. I was tired of it all. So I tossed the pillow to the side and rolled off my bed. This needed to end...*now*. My feet hit the floor with a thud, and I shuffled toward my bedroom door. The door creaked on its hinges when I opened it. I peered around the corner down the dark hallway, although I wasn't sure why. I knew they were in their bedroom. It was on the other side of my wall.

As I approached the door to their room, I saw the shining steel blade I carried in my hand, and I was aware of what I had to do. The doorknob turned freely. *They hadn't even locked the door.*

"Get off her right now!" I stood firm across from my mom and the jackass of a man that lived with us.

"Sweetie, this doesn't concern you. Go back to bed." *Was*

she serious? Like I could sleep through the deafening sounds of my mom's boyfriend beating the crap out of her.

"What do you think you're going to do with that, Alexis?" He chuckled a throaty laugh with his rotten teeth on display. Both his cold laugh and his dental disaster made me want to vomit. I choked down the burning bile that threatened to travel its sour contents up my throat.

Before I could answer the bastard, the door behind me flew open, and a man donned in a dark cape appeared in the room. I twisted on my heels to get a good look at the masked man that materialized like a magic spell. My mom's boyfriend found the distraction opportunistic and grabbed the knife from my hand and proceeded to stab at the stranger. I was horrified as it all played out in slow motion before me, and he lunged toward the unknown visitor and impaled the blade into him.

The man collapsed with a thud and tugged at my nightgown, taking me down with him, pulling me on top of him when he fell. There was only the dimly lit moon outside the window illuminating the room, so I couldn't identify the crazy man who'd just broken into our house.

"Butterfly. I was trying to save you."

But I recognized that voice. Desperately yanking the mask off the man's face, I gaped in bewilderment as those hazel eyes looked at me for only a moment before the life drained out of them. Those amazing eyes that once stared right into my soul were lifeless.

I couldn't breathe. Choking sobs scratched at my throat, and a wave of panic surrounded me. My vision blurred and contorted. The walls, the floor, the ceiling, the whole room spun as the oxygen began to deplete, and a sheet of darkness slipped a veil over my eyes. I hadn't a clue of what to do.

I tightly squeezed my eyes shut, and when I cautiously opened them again, my heart pounded in my ears and palpitations were flying through my chest. If it was possible for someone's heart to take flight, mine was certainly beating fast enough to burst right out of my chest. But when I surveyed my environment throughout the blanket of darkness, I realized I was in my apartment, in my bed. I wasn't at my mom's house.

I swallowed the despair, and I felt a wretchedness I had never experienced before. I needed to find out if Cam was okay. Fighting against my cloudy state of mind, I desperately sought out his number in my phone and called him. I could have sent him a text, but I needed to hear his voice. I had just gotten my childhood hero back.

"Butterfly?" Hearing the soft sound of his sleepy voice was the reassurance I needed, but I had no idea what to say to him. Even if I could transcribe thoughts into words, I wasn't able to speak. I still felt like the wind had been knocked out of me, and a suffocating sensation tightened in my throat.

"Are you okay?" The volume of his tone increased, and he sounded more awake now.

Still fighting through the cobwebs of my nightmare-filled sleep, my voice remained silent, and reckless shuddering took hold of my core. It was another beat before I realized I was sobbing. So much for not falling apart in front of him. At least he couldn't see me.

"I'm on my way over to your place; I'll be there in ten minutes." His blunt comment jarred me back to reality.

"I had a bad dream, and I just needed to know you were okay." I hiccupped while I continued the struggle to find my voice between sobs.

"And now I need to know *you're* okay, so I'll be there soon." The ignition of his truck fired, and his engine roared to life on his end of the line. *He had left his apartment that quickly?*

"That's not necessary, Cam. I'm fine. It was just a bad dream. I'm sorry I woke you." Fearful the edginess of my tone was reflected in the wavering of my voice, I ended the call and sniffed back more tears.

It was only a second before I saw his name and number scroll across my phone. I didn't answer. I wasn't going to answer. *What have I done?* I shouldn't have called him. I hadn't had a nightmare in a really long time. It caught me off guard, and before I realized what I was doing, I'd called him. Now he was on his way over.

Alexis: I'm fine, really. Please don't come over.

Cam: See you soon :-)

Crap.

Maybe I just wouldn't answer the door when he got here.

The knocking started softly at first but then increased in intensity, and soon, he spoke with desperation and need along with the pounding. "Lex, open the door, please. Lex, open up, please."

I glanced at my phone. Two thirteen. He'd end up waking everyone on this floor if I didn't answer him, so I had no choice but to let him in. After unlatching the deadbolt and slightly turning my knob, I forced myself to take a step back from the door swinging inward with a heavy shove.

Without even giving me a second to adjust to his intense presence, his arms were wrapped around me. *Didn't he know that I hated hugs?* But he was trying to comfort me. I pressed my hands against his firm chest and pushed him away. His penetrating gaze drove me to take an additional step backward.

"I just had a bad dream. You didn't need to come over here and rescue me like I'm some kind of damsel in distress."

He kicked my door shut behind him with his flip-flop-clad foot. "I didn't come over here to rescue you. I came over because my friend needed me." Then he patted his chest and thighs. "I forgot the Kit Kats, though."

Okay, so that made me laugh a little. "I don't need a Kit Kat every time I get upset." The tightened muscles in my neck and back uncoiled and released some of the tension that my dream had stirred up.

"Come on." He offered his hand, and God help me, I took it. He led me down the narrow hall and into my room. "Lay back down, and I'll sit with you until you fall asleep."

"This is silly." I attempted to pull away from his grasp, but he firmly held on. He was so incredibly strong.

He kicked off his flip-flops and pulled me toward my bed with him. "Go ahead and get under the covers." He released me at that point so I could slide beneath my butterfly comforter. Yes. I was a grown woman, and I had butterflies on my quilt cover.

The mattress dipped with his weight as he sat next to me on top of the covers. He raked his fingers through my hair, causing a tingling sensation on my scalp, and I gave into the relaxation from his touch.

"Do you want to talk about your dream?"

I shook my head.

"Okay. But just so you know, I'm a great listener."

I didn't respond with words, but I was pretty sure I moaned slightly as he continued to stroke my hair. A yawn escaped as sleepiness surrounded my body and mind rather quickly, and before too long, my slumber ensued.

I woke up to the sound of talking. It was daylight in my room, and I could hear voices coming from the front of my apartment. I recognized Cam's immediately, but I was unsure of who he was speaking with. Not even thinking to brush my teeth or hair, I crept out of my bedroom and down the hall listening to the conversation as I quietly treaded on the carpet.

"Yes, MommaRita. Lean Bean and I will be there. And I want to bring a friend, too."

"I already heard about Travis. Claudette asked if your friend could come over, too." He either had his phone on speaker, or this woman was the loudest phone talker ever.

"I wasn't talking about Travis. I want to bring a girl." Then the sound of deafening squealing and high-pitched screeching pierced the air as Cam came into my view. He pulled the phone away from his ear at the offensive noise. As he swiveled his head, he noticed me standing in the hallway. He mouthed *Sorry* and continued his conversation.

"My little Cameron is finally bringing a girl over to our house. I'm so happy, I not sure how I'll be able to contain my excitement until tomorrow. What's her name?"

"Her name is Alexis. She works with Lean Bean."

"Oooh, so she's a nurse?"

"Yes. And we're just getting to know each other, so don't go planning a wedding or anything. Besides, she just wants to be friends."

"Well, that won't last. You're handsome and charming. You'll win her heart over before long, sweetheart. Tell her I'm thrilled beyond words to have her over for dinner tomorrow."

"All right, MommaRita. I will, but I have to go. Love you."

"Love you, too. See you tomorrow."

He ended his call and continued to stare at me. "I'm sorry. My mother is very loud on the phone. I have to remember to turn the volume back up after we're done talking, otherwise, I can't hear anyone else who calls me."

"Does she always speak that loudly, or is it just when she's on the phone? I'd like to have an idea what I'm in for since you told her I was going to her house for dinner without even asking me yet." We both stood in our respective spots. He in my living room, and me at the edge of the hallway.

"Will you please go with me to dinner at my parents' house tomorrow? Charlie will be there. And Louis. And Claudette. And apparently, Travis." He shook his head as if trying to wrap his mind around that.

"I'll think about it." I shrugged and began to retreat to my bedroom. His footsteps followed behind me.

"Butterfly, trust me. You'll want to go. My mother is an amazing cook. You won't want to miss out on her culinary magic." That did sound tempting.

I whipped my head back around to face him once I had re-entered my room. *What is he doing in here anyway? How is it possible that he feels like it's okay for him to be in my personal space just like that?* "What's with the 'MommaRita'? Is there a story there? And what about Lean Bean?"

He took a seat on the edge of the mattress and chuckled. I continued to stand, taking in how comfortable he appeared in my room.

"My mother's name is Rita. So you can call her that. Or Mrs. C. That's what Louis calls her. But don't call her Mrs. Callahan. She hates when adults do that." He slid back toward the headboard and stretched his long legs out in front of him. Then he padded the area next to him. As if it was the most natural thing to do, I instinctively slid into the spot next to him. "When I was five or six, my mother was going out to have some drinks with her friends. They were going to have margaritas, but I thought she had said momma-ritas. I thought there was a drink named after her, so I started calling her MommaRita. She thought it was adorable, so it stuck. Louis and Charlie have always teased me and called me a momma's boy. Maybe I am. Technically,

I'm the youngest, and I'm the only boy, so she's always had a soft spot for me."

"Which means you could get away with murder." The irony of my statement almost made me shudder. I had meant for the comment to be lighthearted, but given the dream I had last night, I felt my insides begin to churn.

"I guess it's fair to say that I tended to get away with more than the girls. My mom always said it was my hazel eyes. My sisters have blue and gray ones. MommaRita said that the hazel ones are magic. She said I have the same eyes as my dad and when she looks into them, she is totally hypnotized and can be manipulated into anything." He shrugged indifferently.

"So that's Batman's superpower? Hypnotic eyes? I guess I better not stare too long, or you'll get me to do all kinds of crazy things." I was inexperienced at flirting, but I was pretty sure that I may have sounded like I was doing just that.

Cam leaned toward me, and my heart turned over in response. When my phone vibrated on my nightstand, I reflexively jumped. Still startled, I released my cell from the charging cable and viewed the name on my screen.

"Hey, Charlie," I answered while watching Cam roll his eyes and flop back on my bed.

"How do you feel about shopping?"

I wasn't sure what she was asking. I needed clarification. "You mean, like, for groceries?"

She snickered on the other end of the line. "You are just like me. No, I mean for clothes. Like trying on outfits at stores in the mall and then spending too much money."

"It's not really my thing, why?"

"I have to go to a firehouse awards banquet with Louis, and I need a new dress. Please come with me! I'll take you to lunch afterward. I absolutely *hate* shopping for dresses. I don't want to go by myself, and if I ask Claudette, she'll make me look for accessories, and I'll end up with a manicure and a makeover. Please save me from that torture!"

I could understand the whole misery loves company mentality. "Okay. I'll go. What time should I meet you?" I wasn't even sure what time it was. I hadn't glanced at the clock before I walked into my living room this morning.

"I'll pick you up in a half-hour. Can you be ready by then?"

"Yep. See you soon." I ended the call with Charlie and then observed her brother still laying on my bed with his hands covering his eyes. "You need to go. I don't want your sister finding out that you spent the night at my place."

He removed his hands from his face and sat upright. "I guess I should explain that Charlie—or as I call her, *Lean Bean*—and I don't have secrets from each other. I won't tell her right now, but I will eventually. Because she's my best friend, and she is going to want to be told about every detail with Butterfly girl. If you spend the day with her, she'll be probing you for information, too. And you'll likely give it to her, because she's a good friend, and you'll want to tell her."

"So you're saying, everything I share with you will go to your sister." I wasn't sure how I felt about that.

"If there's something you don't want me to tell her, I'll keep it to myself. I should rephrase. I don't *usually* keep secrets from her. But I can assure you that Lean Bean and I are the best secret keepers you will ever meet."

"Is the reason you call your sister Lean Bean a secret?"

He flashed his megawatt smile at me and let out the cutest chuckle. "Uh…no. I couldn't pronounce Charlene when I was little, so I called her Lean. At some point, I added Bean, and that's how it's been ever since."

"So you have a nickname for your mom and your twin sister…"

"And you," he interjected before I finished my thought.

"What about Claudette? You have a nickname for her, too?"

"Nah. I just call her Claude. She and I didn't exactly get along very well when we were growing up. She hated being called Claude, so that's why I did it." He slid closer to me. "I only have nicknames for the most important women in my life."

My heart ascended into my throat, so I choked it back down. I wasn't exactly sure what he was saying. *Does he mean I'm one of the most important women in his life?* We hardly knew each other anymore. I was aware that he wanted to get reacquainted again, but I certainly wasn't ready to tell him about my past.

I finally convinced Cam to leave my apartment so I could get ready to go shopping with Charlie. She picked me up just as promised.

"Thanks for going to the mall with me. I haven't met many girls like me, so I'm usually forced to go on these adventures alone." Charlie looked genuinely happy that I had agreed to tag along. Then again, maybe she was happy for another reason.

"Thanks for asking. I haven't had real friends in a while. This is nice." I returned the smile while sitting in the front seat.

"I'm just ecstatic to have a female friend. I love Louis and my brother, but I can't count on them to give me an honest opinion when it comes to shopping. They'd say everything looks great just to get out of the store faster," she scoffed.

"It sounds like you have done the whole shopping excursion a time or two with them before?"

"Unfortunately, yes."

We went to several different stores, and Charlie tried on a dozen dresses. She finally decided on a long, flowing black dress with a low-cut bodice and tapered waist. She looked amazing in it. I was sure that Louis would love it. After that, we went to get some lunch. We left the mall and visited a restaurant across the highway from the shopping center.

"So I can't keep it in any longer." She sat across from me in a booth after we placed our order with the waitress. "I know you're Butterfly."

I must have let my astonishment overtake my expression because I was truly taken aback by her abrupt comment. "Okay?" I figured she had more to say about the topic.

"And Cam said you just want to be friends, which is absolutely fine. But I just wanted to tell you that I have never seen him so into a girl before." That bit of information actually made me do a little internal happy dance.

"So he told you I was the girl from the school bus?" He had said he told her everything.

"Please." She let out a slight giggle. "I figured it out the same time he did. Of course, I had to fill Louis in later. He didn't put two and two together as easily. Plus, Cam and I have a little bit of a twin vibe between us. It sounds weird, but we're very in tune with each other. He can sometimes tell what I'm thinking before I do." She laughed again.

I enjoyed hearing about her relationship with her brother. They were such good friends, and Louis seemed to fit well into their dynamic. I couldn't imagine another man being so accepting of the special bond those two had. I could see a different boyfriend being jealous of the closeness the twins had. I envied that connection. I certainly appreciated that they both wanted to include me in a friendship.

"He invited me to your parents' house for dinner tomorrow." My inner teenager felt a little like I was confessing to my friend about a secret crush who had just asked me out on a date.

"Oh, I've heard. My mother called me right after I spoke to you this morning. I could barely understand what she was saying between all the squealing." She leaned forward, resting her elbows on the table to move closer to me. "She's more than a little excited that my brother, the ever bachelor, is bringing a girl home to meet Mom and Dad. She'll probably hug, kiss, and squeeze you to pieces. I hope it doesn't scare you off."

"I appreciate the warning." *How in the world am I going to survive that? I can't stand to let someone hug and kiss me. Maybe I should rethink this whole dinner-with-the-parents thing.*

I drew in a quick, sharp breath as I grappled with the sudden onset of anxiety. I couldn't erase the panic I was sure I wore across my face and wreaked havoc within my body. Perspiration oozed out of my pores, causing a cool, clammy sensation along my skin.

"Are you okay, Alexis? You look pale and diaphoretic. If you weren't so young, I'd be worried you were having a heart attack."

Maybe I was. My throat was dry. My hands were sweaty. I felt lightheaded. Maybe this was what a heart attack felt like. "I guess I'm just not a touchy-feely type of person," I managed to squeak out.

"Well, I'll just tell my mom to keep her hands to herself." Her expression was serious and stoic. "And don't worry, I already told my brother to keep his hands to himself." Then a smile broke across her face. She got me. I may not have had many friends over the span of my life, but if I had to wait until now to end up with the Callahan twins, it was worth it. Maybe I had finally come across people who understood me, and that realization calmed my fears.

The clouds hung dark and low in the sky, indicating a summer thunderstorm was about to unleash. I managed to escape from Charlie's car into my apartment before being pelted by an outpouring of thunderous rain pellets. I wasn't inside my place very long before there was a gentle knocking on my door. After peering out the peephole, I discovered that I had left one Callahan twin only to have another show up at my apartment.

"What are you doing here, Cam?" I asked as I flung the door open. It really had only been a few hours since I had last seen him.

He pushed my door open beyond my grasp and eased his way in just as he had done previously. "I understand that you hate surprises. We've established that I need to be better about arriving unannounced, but I wanted to see you, Butterfly." He turned to face me and held up a DVD. "We still haven't watched *Batman*. You had said some other time, so here I am." His hair was freshly wet from the storm, and his T-shirt had caught several hundred droplets of rainwater.

He was persistent; I'd give him that. "I figured it'd be more of a mutually established time versus bulldozing your way into another opportunity."

"Oh, you know you can't wait to watch this movie." The devilish grin he displayed was part confident and part sexy.

"It better be Michael Keaton." I was actually super excited to see Cam again, but I didn't want to be obvious. I was confused by my own mixed emotions. I could only imagine what signals I must have given off to him.

"Of course it is. It's the perfect rainy-day activity. We'll watch a DVD, and then if the showers stop, I can take you out to dinner. If it is still downpouring, we can order in."

"Cam, you just left me a few hours ago. Aren't you going

to get tired of spending so much time with me?" I had gotten pretty used to being alone, and these Callahans hadn't left me alone at all today.

"I will never *ever* get tired of spending time with you." Those damn eyes bore a hole right into the pit of my stomach. "If you get tired of *me*, just say the word, and I'll go."

Say *the word.* I couldn't say *any* words. I had always thought it was the fact that Cam was such an attractive man that made me nervous to be around him. But now I realized it was so much more than that. I wanted him back in my life so desperately when I was six years old. Now that he was here fifteen years later, I couldn't seem to stop myself from letting him get close to me. I wasn't sure how all of this was going to work out. I truly didn't share my crap with anyone. My life was full of baggage, and so far, Cam had been patient and hadn't pressured me for any explanations about anything. But with him back, how long would I be able to continue to keep my secrets? These contemplations were what made me nervous now.

I was scared that Cam would find out where I came from, what I had done, and leave me again. I considered myself a strong woman. I dealt with a lot of stuff in my life, but having Batman leave again might be more than I could handle. So now I struggled with clinging onto him and holding on for dear life or keeping him at arm's length. I would have him as part of my life, but not as an essential piece of it. *Who am I kidding?* I was screwed.

"Fine. You can stay." I hoped I didn't regret this. "But I need to tell you something."

Cam cocked his head and jutted out his jaw. Worry creased his brow in anticipation of what I might say.

"I don't want you to get the wrong idea about having you at my apartment. It's just to watch a movie. I am *not* having sex with you."

The frown he had cautiously worn transformed into that sexy-as-hell crooked grin that he must have perfected during puberty because he did it so effortlessly, and it made me gasp. "For someone who says she's not going to have sex with me, you certainly think about it a lot."

I was only standing a few paces from him, but he stepped toward me, closing the distance between us until he stood so close I could smell the rainwater in his hair.

"When I said watch a movie and have dinner, that's what I meant." He brushed my hair off my shoulders, and when he tucked it behind my ear, an unexpected tingling sensation shot up my spine. "If we were to have sex, I'd skip the movie and dinner." He leaned toward me, and I didn't feel one bit afraid of his close proximity. I thought he was going to kiss me, so I licked my lips in expectation. His lips quickly brushed against my forehead, and then he quickly retreated to my living area.

"Uh, Butterfly?"

I had to break free from the buzzed feeling I was savoring in when I heard Cam's voice.

"Where is your DVD player?"

Okay, so he made me laugh. He made me lose my ability to think, and he made me smile. I was in trouble for sure. "I don't have one."

"Then how are we supposed to watch the movie?" Confusion marred his face as his brows drew together and his eyes narrowed.

"It's on Netflix, silly."

He swiped his brow as an exaggerated sign of relief. He really loved his Batman movies.

We settled onto the couch next to each other while the obligatory preview to the movie started. Cam reached across my lap and linked his thumb with mine. I wasn't sure what the very warm feeling that began to stir within my belly was, but it was comforting…and it felt right.

He had been right next to me, but now he was gone. I knew we were next to each other on the couch, and Cam was holding my hand in our special way. But now it had gotten dark. I must have fallen asleep during the movie. The glare from my television provided enough light for me to see in my dark living room. I was alone on my couch. *Maybe Cam had gotten up to use the bathroom? Maybe he had gone to get food?* I remembered him saying if it was raining, he'd order take-out. *But why didn't he tell me he was leaving?* When I heard knocking, I didn't even bother to look through the peephole. It had to be Cam. He probably went and picked up dinner.

However, when I opened the door, a man who I hadn't seen in over a decade stood on the other side. I attempted to shut the entrance quickly, but he was fast enough to push against the heavy metal. He got his fingers wedged around the jamb, but I didn't care. I wanted him gone, so I slammed the door against his hand in an effort to force him to release his hold.

"Get out of here! I don't want to see you ever again!" I yelled as I shoved my door shut, cracking against his now bleeding knuckles. I continued to push against his hand, but he used his body weight to press against my door. I wasn't going to be able to keep him out.

"Butterfly!"

I heard Cam's voice, but I still didn't see him. He would surely save me from this asshat.

"Lex!"

Where is he? Why hasn't he gotten here yet? Fatigue was crying throughout my wobbly legs, and my arms were shaking with wariness. I wouldn't be able to hold the door much longer.

Vibrations from the ground shook my apartment. The door pulsated beneath my fingers, and my whole body trembled. *This is a crazy time to have an earthquake.* Maryland hardly ever got earthquakes, but the rippling effects intensified.

"Lex, you're having a bad dream. Open your eyes."

I had no idea that my eyes were closed, so I forced myself to open them. The hazy film faded, and Cam's face came into focus, leaning over me. Not trusting where I was, I glanced around, taking in my surrounding. After a brief survey, I recognized my apartment. Hot, wet tears slid down my face. I couldn't believe that dream had felt so real. Cam pulled me upright into a seated position on the couch and drew me into his chest. I flopped my limp, exhausted body against him while he wrapped his arms around me. I didn't hate the hug at all. I felt safe. He saved me.

"Do you want to tell me about your dream?" he asked as he rocked me gently against his chest and stroked my hair.

I merely shook my head. I was wiped out. I was out of breath and out of words.

"Do you have bad dreams all the time?" He pushed me away only far enough to see my face. I twisted my head away from him so I could divert the glowing amber orbs and their penetrating gaze. "Butterfly, whatever ghosts you have in your past can't hurt you anymore. I'll never ever let anyone or anything hurt you again." He brushed his soft, warm lips against my cheek, but I continued to face away from him. "You don't have to tell me if you're not ready. But I want you to know that I am *not* going anywhere. I'll be here for you always."

I wanted to believe him. I really did. I wanted him to be different than other men and to be able to trust him. I felt myself letting go of those thoughts, and I collapsed against his chest again. The tears slid down my face, but I didn't have the overwhelming feeling to sob. Maybe the tears weren't completely from sadness. Maybe they were partially because I had Batman back. Maybe he would help save me from my memories.

It continued to rain, so we ordered Chinese. I was pleasantly surprised to find out that sesame chicken was Cam's favorite entrée also. Although he preferred fried rice, and I preferred steamed rice, we both loved sesame chicken. I wondered if this was how a relationship started. A man and a woman have similar likes and interests, and they connect with each other. I definitely felt drawn to Cam. I wondered if or when he'd turn into an asshole. Because right now, I couldn't imagine that he would ever hurt me. He even said he would protect me from being hurt by someone else. I would have to convince myself that I was strong enough to walk away if things moved in the wrong direction.

Until recently, I had lived my life alone. I didn't want to let other people into it. I'd finally managed to make something of myself, but what would it cost me in the end? I need to be brave enough to live in the moment. Charlie had been a good friend to me. She was honest, fun, and kind-hearted. She worked with me, so I really didn't want to risk letting anything about my past slip around her. This, of course, meant I couldn't tell Cam about my past, either. He'd already admitted that he told his sister everything.

I looked over at the dark-haired man eating his Chinese food with chopsticks, and I glanced down at my own plate while I was holding a fork. *Lord, I'm boring*. "Hey, Cam, can you teach me how to use those things?"

He moved his chopsticks open and shut with his fingers. "These things?"

I nodded in agreement.

"Of course. You've never used chopsticks before?"

I shook my head.

"Well, all right. This can be another first."

I thought I would see a smile, but he was all matter of fact.

He placed his utensils on his plate and grabbed the other pair of wooden sticks from the wrapper on my breakfast bar where we sat and slipped them out. Then he reached over to grab my hand, placing the slender wooden rods in the proper places with my fingers and thumb. He held my hand and showed me how to maneuver the chopsticks. I practiced with the chicken first and then moved onto the rice. I didn't do very well with the rice. It all wanted to fall apart. The pieces of chicken were easier to grasp. He encouraged me and watched me eat while he left his own food to get cold.

Once he felt fairly confident in my ability of mastering the art of using chopsticks, he resumed eating his own dinner. "So, Butterfly, I was thinking." He talked while shoving food into his mouth. *Didn't his mother ever tell him not to talk with his mouth full?* "I was thinking I would spend the night again."

"Uh…no." Because uh…no.

"Don't worry. Spend the night means just sleeping. No sex." He waggled his brows at me as he continued to chew. "I mean it. I promise, even if you beg me for sex, I absolutely will not have sex with you. Pinky swear."

"No. I'm not letting you spend the night." I was curious about what brought this on, though.

"If you have a nightmare, I'll already be here. It'll save me a trip in the middle of the night." So that's what this was. A humiliating, deflated feeling swirled in my belly.

"I'm so sorry about calling you last night. I hadn't had a nightmare in a really long time, and I guess I got a little freaked out. I won't call you like that again." I gave up on the chopsticks, deciding I was finished eating at that point.

He reached for my hand, and although I felt like I should pull away, I didn't offer much resistance. His face was set in a hard, determined expression contrasted by his soft, pleading voice. "Please call me whenever you need me. Call me whenever you want to. I just want to be with you. I can't explain it. I've never felt like I wanted to see a woman more than I want to see you. I have never—and will never—get tired of seeing or hearing you. I will come over at a moment's notice." He released the light touch from my hand and reached for a stray tendril of hair, but rather than brush it away again and tuck it behind my ear, he twirled it around his finger. "Let me stay tonight. I let you leave my place last night, but please don't make me leave yours tonight."

How am I going to say no? He could probably ask me anything at this moment and I'd give in.

I licked my lips once again, thinking he might kiss me. His gaze encouraged me closer, and I inched my head toward his willingly. Then he broke his stare and looked back at his plate.

What just happened? "So if I let you stay, it's going to be innocent like a slumber party?"

My comment got him to return his attention in my direction. "Oh, hell no. Claudette and her friends used to paint their nails, watch chick flicks, and call boys. They chattered loudly and made high-pitched squealing noises over everything."

"I was never invited to a sleepover when I was a kid, so I wouldn't have any idea what it was really like, other than what I've seen on TV or in movies." No way would I have ever had a friend stay over my childhood house, and being so withdrawn made no one want to reach out to me either.

Cam thunderously clapped his hands together once, startling me from my straying thoughts. "Well, that can be another first then." He stood from his stool and hugged me quickly. "We can eat junk food and ice cream. We can even watch a chick flick if you want."

"Shouldn't I have a slumber party with a girl? Not...well, not...with you?"

"Hey, when I was growing up, Charlie and Louis and I had sleepovers all the time. Boys can have sleepovers with girls." He flashed that mischievous grin in my direction, and my heart rate kicked up a notch.

"I don't know, Cam. I think it's weird...where are you going to sleep?" I gestured around at my small one-bedroom apartment.

"I'll sleep wherever you want me to. And maybe it's weird for Cam. But it's not weird for Batman."

I threw an exaggerated eye roll at him. I really and truly liked him. He'd stayed at my apartment last night. *What's the harm in another night?* Of course I would waver eventually. His irresistible charm had me swimming in a pool of trouble.

"Okay. Batman can stay over...but he better be a good guy and not a villain under that mask." My heart proceeded to engage in tumultuous flip-flops.

"And in the morning, I'll take you to breakfast, and then we can go for a bike ride." He was standing now and cleaning up our dinner remains. He gathered the dishes and scraped the plates. He even put the leftovers in the fridge. My father and certainly my mother's boyfriend had never cleaned a kitchen—or anything remotely domestic.

"Um...Cam..."

He'd think I was weird. One of these times, he would realize how strange I was and give up on the thought of being friends with me.

"Yes, Butterfly." He held his gaze at me for a breathtaking

moment while I tried my best to work up my nerve to confess something embarrassing about myself.

I took a deep breath and turned my face away as I huffed out my comment. "I don't know how to ride a bike."

"Okay. We can ride a surrey on the boardwalk. It's like a bike, but we can sit next to each other on a bench and pedal with our feet. It will be fun. Have you ever done that before?"

Is he kidding?

I shook my head.

"Great! Another first. I'm truly hoping with all the firsts I'm around for that you won't be able to forget me." He approached me while I still sat on my bar stool. Then he tilted his head so close to me that his forehead eventually rested on mine. "But you need to stop doing this."

I licked my lips, unsure of how to respond. "What…what am I doing?"

"You act like you want me to kiss you."

I pulled away slightly. *Was it that obvious?*

A beat later, his hands pulled me back into him, and he kissed the top of my head with a brief peck. "Hey, that's a first that I don't want to rush. Okay?"

Crap. "Will you at least tell me when that's going to be? I've already told you that I *hate* surprises." I felt his Adam's apple move up and down along the side of my head as he laughed.

"Sure. I'll make sure you have a pretty good idea of when it's going to happen." His masculine warmth felt so good against me.

We watched a rom-com and ate popcorn. We opted to stay away from ice cream, deciding to leave that for the next time instead. When I was ready to go to bed, Cam followed me into my bedroom. He promised to sit with me until I fell asleep and then go out to my living room and sleep on the couch. Therefore, I was a little surprised when the light of day filtered through the curtains and there was a shirtless man in my bed next to me.

The warmth of his body pressed against mine, even though I wasn't even facing in his direction. When I shifted my weight, his arm and leg draped across me and pinned me in place. "Hey, Cam?"

"Mhmm." He pulled me into him and cuddled closer to me, if that was even possible.

"Cam!" I had to raise my voice to get him to wake up.

It worked. He bolted upright. I turned over to face him. He rubbed his eyes with the palms of his hands, and his day-old stubble covered his jawline.

"You startled me."

I heard his words, but I was looking at the six-pack ripple of abs staring right at me.

"I'm sorry. You kind of had me pinned. I couldn't move." I no longer wanted to move, actually. I couldn't remember why I wanted him to move away from me, either. I was pretty sure I liked having this beautiful man in my bed. I was also pretty sure he had slept in many other women's beds before mine. It was probably a habit; his motions were just automatic.

My happiness faded, which was most likely apparent to Cam. "Why do you suddenly look sad, Butterfly?" He was fully awake now. "I'm sorry about not moving to the couch last night. I must've fallen asleep."

He must have thought I was upset that he'd slept in my bed, given his explanation. I guess he didn't realize that I'd found myself upset that he had slept in so many other beds.

With a brush of his fingers across my temple, I instinctively pulled away. "Seriously, Lex, what's up?"

I rolled out of bed and began my walk toward the bathroom. Cam's feet hit the ground behind me, and he fell into step as I walked. I swiftly whirled around to address his close presence. "Cam, I'm going to the bathroom. I don't want you following me."

He really didn't deserve the cold shoulder I was giving him, but I needed a second to breathe again. So I splashed water on my face and brushed my teeth. When I felt ready to confront him again, I stepped back into my bedroom, but he wasn't there. I walked the few steps toward my living room when I saw his broad shoulders covered in a T-shirt and his back to me.

"I'm sorry I snapped at you this morning."

He held his position for a beat before turning around to respond to my comment. His dark hair was tousled, and I swear, he totally rocked the just-rolled-out-of-bed look. "I just figured you weren't a morning person."

I expected a smile after his comment, but his face continued to hold a serious expression.

"Waking up with you in my bed was a little awkward." I dug deep to extract the courage prior to expelling my insightful opinion, or more accurately, before saying something I prepared to regret fly out of my mouth. "I'm sure you're used to waking up next to a woman, but I'm *not* used to waking up next to a man."

Okay, so now he smiled. That delightfully amazing, sexy, playful grin that I was sure would have any woman wanting to go to bed with him, stretched out effortlessly across his chiseled features, even creasing the outer corners of his hazel eyes. "I don't make it a habit of waking up next to a woman. Honestly, I have never wanted to spend the night with a woman before."

"But you've spent the last two nights with me." *What the hell am I doing?*

"Yeah, I guess I should've said that I have never wanted to spend the night with a woman before *now*."

My heart rate accelerated, and my mouth absolved of any moisture. I had to swallow that dry lump pretty forcefully as his bare feet carried him to me. His super masculine presence invaded my personal space without physically touching me. So when he placed his hands on my waist, a quiet gasp escaped me. And when he pulled me toward him, I couldn't find my ability to put distance between us again. My breasts bumped into his hard chest with a soft thump, knocking me off balance, initiating my whole weight to crash against him. My cheek rested against him until he stroked the bottom of my chin with his finger, urging me to look up at him.

He leaned down. His six-foot-plus frame towered over my five-foot-five body. "I'm hoping you feel the same about me. I want you to tell me that you've never wanted to spend the night with a man before now, and you have never wanted to wake up next to a man before now." His throaty, masculine voice caused those butterflies to flutter their wings against the lining of my stomach again, while my lady parts flooded with warmth and tingly sensations.

"Are you going to kiss me now?" My voice was barely a whisper, because I couldn't seem to choke out the words.

"Is that okay with you?" His swirling amber-colored orbs searched mine with a fiery desire and longing.

I nodded eagerly. *Hell, yes!*

"Then I'm going to kiss the hell out of you, Butterfly."

He was right. From the moment his lips collided with mine—even before that—I envisioned this was going to be the best kiss I'd ever had in my life. It would most likely be the best kiss I *would* ever have in my life. His lips were soft, but his day-old stubble scratched against my face as he kissed and sucked on my lips. When his tongue urged my mouth open, I gladly complied with the unspoken request. His silky tongue skillfully explored every part of the warmth inside of my mouth.

His large hands cupped the sides of my face, sending scorching heat through my cheeks. I wanted him closer to me, so I awkwardly wrapped my arms around his neck, pressing myself against him. The increased contact caused the warmth to spread throughout my entire body. The simmering heat transformed to a full boil, and soon, I was perspiring. He certainly wouldn't find that very attractive. Self-consciousness and embarrassment pounded in my head. I tried to pull away, but he kept me close to him.

My brain shouted, my lady parts sang, my heart thumped, and my lungs struggled to get enough air. That's what finally caused me to break free from that amazing, time-freezing kiss. I needed a moment to collect myself. Apparently, he did, too. His breathing was rapid and shallow. I had seen hyperventilation before, but it was smoking hot on him. His eyes begged for my patience. So I waited, which allowed me the opportunity to regain my own composure as he took several, quick gasps before speaking.

"I've tried to keep things platonic, Lex. I really have. But I'm so drawn to you. It's like this invisible force that is more powerful than me. I don't… I won't press things on you that you aren't ready for. I really don't want you to feel pressured into anything. I promise, I'll be okay with just being around you."

"I wanted you to kiss me, Cam." I dropped my gaze, like I often did when I was embarrassed. "I'm not like you. I'm awkward and self-conscious. And I'm still trying to figure a lot of things out."

With the delicate touch of a feather, his soft lips brushed against my forehead. "Butterfly, you're amazing. You're mysterious and warm and caring. I'm fascinated by the fact that you are so innocent at times, but also a total badass that carries a switchblade. I want to be around you all the time."

Well, damn. What am I supposed to say to that? His comment gave me enough of a confidence boost to pull my eyes back up at his and boldly connect back to his.

"So where do we go from here?" I was definitely moving into uncharted territory. I loved being around him, but I was also aware someone like him had the ability to hurt me…*a lot.*

"We're going to continue to get to know each other. We'll continue to spend time together, and we'll see where things go…okay?"

I merely nodded. *How can one person have such an influence on my actions?* I really think I would've agreed to anything he said. I wasn't sure how I was so willing to give a man that much control over me.

"One of these days, I'm going to convince you to trust me, and you'll let me in because we are friends, right?"

Sure, we were friends, but as far as letting him into the secrets of my past…well, that just wasn't going to happen. He might have control over some of my actions, but he wouldn't be able to penetrate that wall of steel around the crap from my previous life. I didn't even go there if I could possibly help it. That area of me was kept locked up tight.

"But I have never dated a friend before, so you may need to be a little patient with me. I'm not sure how to blend the two together yet."

I appreciated his honesty, although it almost sounded like a premonition that he would screw things up and hurt me in the process. Those invading thoughts forced my back to straighten. However, my stiff posture relaxed slightly when he pulled me close to him again, because "dated a friend" still resonated in my ears.

"So we're…dating?" I wasn't sure why I felt like I needed

to push him away, but there I was, using my hands against his chest to wedge extra space between us. I needed to protect myself from him for reasons I couldn't quite put my finger on. Maybe it was that comment he made about me letting him in. Into what? My mind, my heart, my past? The first two quite possibly...but the third...not going to happen.

"You're adorable. Of course we're dating. We have been for a while." His smile was playful yet comforting. "Ever since you agreed to go to breakfast with me after your shift that day. I mean, Charlie and Travis were there, too, but I still count that as our first date."

Definitely uncharted territory. I doubted that I had *ever* dated anyone before. I'd never had any interest in spending a whole lot of time with boys when I was younger, or men when I was older. Cam was the only boy I wanted to be around when I was a little girl. And now that I'd grown up, he was the only man I wanted to be around again. Louis and Travis seemed like okay guys, too. Maybe Cam was changing my whole perspective on men in general. *How can one person change my whole belief in mankind?*

"So I'd like to call you my girlfriend now, if that's okay with you."

Really? He could call me whatever he wanted. Any name he said broke my skin out in gooseflesh. When I heard Lex in that throaty voice of his, I found it sexy as hell. When the name Butterfly passed his lips, I felt my heart up in my throat. Now that he wanted to call me his girlfriend, I might just melt into a puddle on the floor.

"Are you with me?"

So maybe I drifted off in my own head for a moment. *What happened to that wall I need to protect myself?* "What does that title even mean?"

He let a small laugh escape and attempted to pull me

toward him again trying to close the gap I had created. "It means we're only dating each other."

"Okay." I liked that, because the thought of him with another woman made me vomit a little in my mouth. *Who needs that wall, anyway? I have several walls in place. Just because I let one or two come tumbling down doesn't mean I can't keep that one around my past sealed shut.*

"Well, okay then. Go ahead and get ready, so I can take my girlfriend to breakfast and spend the day with her."

It sounded like the perfect plan to me.

8
CAMERON

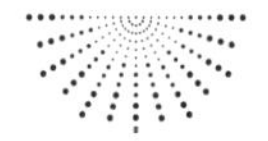

Since I planned to ride a surrey on the boardwalk, I took my *girlfriend* to a breakfast diner on the way to the beach. It felt weird to give Lex that title, but at the same time, it felt good. Even though I hadn't used that term in a really long time, it seemed completely appropriate for what we had with each other. I haven't even had a girlfriend since Cassidy Crandell in eleventh grade. She'd wanted that label since we had sex, so I figured I'd oblige her. I wasn't in love, so of course it didn't work out. I was seventeen and horny. I would have probably called her my wife if it meant I could continue to have sex with her.

Honestly, I'd only had physical relationships with women I was interested in since then. Lex was different, though. I loved to spend time with her, whether anything physical happened or not. Don't get me wrong, I would've loved to hold her naked in my bed, but I was crazy happy just being in the same room as her.

I loved how she wore a ponytail at the nape of her neck so I could see her exposed skin. I loved that her blue eyes said so many things without her mouth having to utter a word.

And I loved that she only smiled when she was truly content, and not just to be flirtatious. Of course, she didn't even have to flirt to get my pulse racing.

Having such an emotional investment in a woman was foreign to me. Of course I wanted both the emotional connection *and* the physical intimacy. But I wouldn't even begin to have a clue how to go about that. I needed some advice. So I sent a text to the group chat I had with my two best friends while she used the restroom.

Cam: How did you two go from friends to boyfriend/girlfriend status?

Louis: Are you looking for advice or a really long, boring story?

Charlie: HEY!

Cam: Advice, I guess.

Charlie: [jumping up and down GIF]

Louis: If it feels right, everything will fall into place.

Charlie: [heart emoji]

Cam: Are you going to just text me GIFs and emojis Lean Bean?

Charlie: [laughing emoji]

Cam: Why do I even bother? [hand slapping me in the forehead emoji]

Louis: Are you planning to ask Alexis to be your girlfriend?

Cam: I already did.

Charlie: What did she say? What did she say?

Cam: I don't think I want to tell you two now.

Charlie: Oh come on! Please! Tell us!

Louis: Please!

Cam: You two are pathetic. Maybe I should start the silent game.

Charlie: Okay. I lose. I owe you a soda. #tellmeplease

Cam: She said YES

Louis: [heart for eyes emoji]

Charlie: [big heart emoji]

Cam: Gotta go. She's walking back from the bathroom now…and she looks upset. Hopefully I haven't screwed things up already.

Louis: TTYL

Charlie: See you at Mom & Dad's

"We have to go right now, Cam." She hadn't even reached our table before she blurted that sentence out. Her brow was outlined with a frazzled expression. Her creamy complexion had gone pale, and her body was trembling.

I reached for her hands and pulled her to the chair next to me at the table. "What's wrong, Lex?" Worry coursed through me as I held her palms that were moist with perspiration as her trembling intensified. I hadn't seen her upset like this since that nightmare she had a few nights ago. I was aware that she had secrets in her past she wasn't comfortable talking to me about, but I was pretty sure she would confide in me one day. I just needed to be patient.

"Alexis. Don't you dare walk away from me! I'm talking to you." The roar of an older, gruff voice boomed throughout the restaurant.

"Please, Cam. I want to go." Hysteria shuddered through her panic-laced speech. Her eyes glistened with unshed tears, and the begging plea was insistent.

I wanted to take her hurt away, but I also wanted to know what I was up against.

"Alexis!" I heard the same voice, but at an increasing cadence just before I saw the short, balding man with gray wisps of hair stomp toward our table.

I stood to my full height and reluctantly released Lex's hands.

"Hey, I don't want any trouble. She obviously doesn't want to speak with you, so I think it's best if you leave her alone." My upright stance drew an angry scowl across the old guy's face.

"I wasn't speaking to you, asshole. I'm talking to her." He lunged forward, toward my Butterfly, but being half his age, I was quicker on my feet than he was.

I grabbed his arm and had it twisted behind his back before he had a chance to touch her. "Like I said before, she isn't interested. It's time for you to go. You can leave on your own, or I'm happy to assist you. It's your call." I held a firm grasp on his arm while he fought against me. He was no match for my strength, but he attempted to struggle out of my hold, nonetheless. Now would be a great time to break his arm. Louis was always the bigger person. He could walk away from a fight, but not me. I was always happy to show a jackass my fist.

"Fine. I'll leave." I shoved the old guy away from us, and he stumbled forward. He coughed, and with one last look, he walked in the opposite direction. I let him go. I didn't want Lex to see that angry side of me. Louis would have been proud.

I sat back down next to Lex. "Who the hell was that retched old man?"

"That was my dad." She threw herself at me at that moment, so all I could do was catch her and wrap my arms around her. I had so many questions. I'd tried to be respectful of her privacy, but I might have to start asking more about her past sooner rather than later.

I managed to pay our check, collect Lex in her fragile state, and walk her out to my truck. After helping her into the passenger seat, I swiftly jogged to the driver's side and slipped behind the steering wheel. Once I started the ignition, I returned my arm to its proper place wrapped around her shoulder and pulled her toward me.

She sniffled into my T-shirt as I pulled out of the parking lot and onto the highway. I decided to head to the beach, even though I was unsure if this unexpected meeting would alter our plans for the afternoon.

"Butterfly, please talk to me," I whispered into her hair. I had my chin resting on the top of her head and placed a kiss on her light brown hair.

"He's the reason I didn't want to go home every day from school." She spoke into my chest rather than looking at me. I should have punched the asshole when I had the chance.

"Did he…hurt you?" I braced myself for what she might or might not share.

She stiffened at my question and turned her body away as much as she could with the restriction of her seatbelt and stared out the window.

I reached over and linked my thumb with hers, reminding her of who I was. I wanted to remind her of who we were together. I was her Batman, and she was my Butterfly.

"He used to beat my mom."

My breakfast sank like a brick in my stomach, and my grip tightened on the steering wheel. I wanted to turn my truck around and find that jackass. I took a deep breath and probably gritted my teeth so hard the thousands of dollars my parents had invested into my smile was probably just destroyed. She didn't need me to be a crazy, raging animal. She needed me to comfort her and exhibit patience and understanding. So I unlinked my thumb and grazed the top of her thigh closest to me.

"But he never hit you?" Again, I braced myself for her response.

"No. But I was so terrified of him." Her tone wavered

with a mixture of sadness and perhaps a hint of fear. "I guess I still am."

"Butterfly, I will *never* let anyone hurt you. I wish I had known all those years ago. I would've done anything I could to help you." My heart broke for her. It was ripping apart for the little girl who used to sit next to me on the bus every day. I wished I had been more persistent in asking why she didn't want to go home.

She continued to gaze at the passing trees along the highway. "You couldn't have done anything. You were just a kid."

"My dad's a pediatrician, and my mom is an attorney. I could've had them help you." I needed to hold her again. I couldn't continue to drive. I needed to look into those blue eyes and show her the promise that I would never hurt her. I would never let anyone hurt her. So I pulled into the parking lot of a strip mall.

Placing my truck's gearshift into park, I unbuckled my seat belt and reached across to unbuckle hers, too. Linking my thumb with hers, I slid toward her and placed a peck on her cheek. "Butterfly, I am so sorry."

She wore the saddest expression I'd ever seen. She wasn't just sad; disappointment washed over her features. She was crushed. *What the hell?*

"I never told anyone about that. I have never shared that part of my past with anyone." She appeared completely shattered. She definitely didn't look like someone relieved to spill a secret kept hidden for so long.

"You can tell me anything. Anything at all, and I won't share it with a soul. I promise." I couldn't stay apart from her for another second. I released the hold our thumbs had, and I pulled her into me. I rubbed her back, and she sank into my chest, collapsing against me in a loud whoosh.

"But you tell Charlie everything." She was whispering, which meant she was worried what my response would be.

"This conversation is only between the two of us. Okay?" I would keep any secret she told me if it meant she'd open up some more. *How could I have not known what was going on back then?* "You don't need to be scared of him anymore. He can't hurt you."

She shifted in her seat, and those beautiful blue eyes found mine. "I was caught off guard. I haven't seen him in so long."

"When was the last time you saw him?" The terror embedded in her face seemed so fresh that I assumed he had made a recent departure from her life.

"He left my mom and me when I was around ten."

I was relieved yet still concerned because she still feared him now. Her traumatizing experience seemed recent. She had a nightmare a few nights ago. *Has she been having nightmares all these years?*

"Cam, I'm totally exhausted. Is it okay if we skip the boardwalk? I really am wiped out." Her flushed face and puffy eyes emphasized her point. I could destroy the person who did this to her.

"Of course, Butterfly. I'll take you home."

Lex was already asleep when I pulled into the parking lot of her apartment complex. "Hey, Lex, we're home." I rubbed her head, standing outside of the passenger door.

She released a soft moan before her eyelids lifted. She practically rolled out of my truck but managed to land on her feet before shuffling toward her apartment.

I walked alongside her, but I held her tightly to me with my arm around her shoulders. I thought she would need to lean on me a little, but she seemed able to walk independently without my assistance.

She fumbled with her keys trying to open her door, so I assisted her. But once inside her apartment, she trudged to her bedroom without saying a word. Of course I followed after placing her keys on the end table in her living room.

I watched her slip under her covers and lay her head on her pillow. I crawled in next to her but remained on top of the comforter. I pressed my body against hers. She faced away from me, so I wrapped my arm around her, effectively spooning her.

"Cam, I kind of want to be alone."

"I want to respect you and give you what you want...but I really feel like you need me. And I want to be here for you," I said into her ponytail.

"I don't think I like the person I am around you." She took a long exhale after that confession.

"What do you mean?"

She flipped over so that we faced each other, but I still was able to keep my arm draped around her waist.

"I feel weak and vulnerable...like I need you. These are not things I'm accustomed to. I'm used to taking care of myself and handling things on my own. Quite honestly, I don't like feeling as if I might need someone." Those blue eyes signaled that she had more to say.

"Butterfly, everyone needs someone sometimes. Hell, I need a lot of people." I brushed the stray hair that had escaped the confines of her ponytail and tucked it behind her ear. "I need Charlie and Louis and my parents. And my God, I need you. I need you so bad I can't even think straight."

She actually blushed. A pink hue darkened her cheeks, and it was the most adorable, honest reaction I had ever seen on a woman. "Cam, some of the things you say make me very uncomfortable."

My feelings bounced back and forth between desire and lust to protectiveness and wanting to hold her and assure her that she was safe. "Butterfly, I have no idea what you must have lived through in your life. But what you need to realize is that not everyone is going to hurt you. I will never purposely hurt you. I get that you've been hurt, but I'll never let anyone hurt you again. I swear it. You will always be safe with me. Just please, let me in." My eyes searched hers as we laid facing each other.

"I've already let you in more than anyone else in my life." She closed her eyes and flipped over to face away from me again.

"And I feel absolutely privileged that you chose to confide in me." Running my fingers through the silky hair of her ponytail was the only comforting measure I could adequately do from that position. "Butterfly, I will share all my secrets with you just to hear one of yours." I wanted her to feel protected and secure with me.

"My secret is that I don't like to share secrets." Exhaustion and defeat seeped out in her whispered remark.

I needed to do something to lift her spirits. So I did what Louis, Charlie, and I used to do to lighten a mood that became too serious. I jabbed my finger into her side and then poked her in the armpit and abdomen. She jerked backward and forward, and then the sweetest sound escaped her. She had a full, throaty laugh.

"Stop, Cam!" she yelled between gasping fits of laughter.

I relented, of course, and pulled on her waist to urge her to roll in my direction and face me again. She beamed a wide smile at me. The most perfect lips curled up in the corners, and I finally saw happiness radiate from her. Pure exhilaration rushed through me as I witnessed her delight. "I like this look on you."

"What, tousled hair and emotional exhaustion?" Those mirth-filled blue eyes sparkled, and her cheekbones were raised and prominent because she was still smiling at me through her sarcasm.

"No. That blissful, happy look." I wanted to bask in her contentment so I could maintain that comforting warmth shooting through every vein in my body. Those soothing thoughts struck my brain with an idea. "Hey, since we didn't make it to the beach, why don't we go to the pool? My gym has a great outdoor pool. We could go there for a while before getting ready for dinner at my parents' house."

And just like that, her smile evaporated. "Cam, I can't swim."

"You can't swim?" I had repeated her because I really couldn't believe it.

"I never learned how." Not only had her happiness taken a hasty exit, but embarrassment had also entered the room.

I didn't want her to feel ashamed. I guess I didn't hide my shock very well. "So we took you in a canoe, and you can't swim?" Guilt sank into my stomach. *How could I have been so presumptuous?*

"I wore a life vest. And besides, I trusted that if something happened, none of you would have let me drown."

Bile crept up my throat, and I had to swallow it back down. Guilt did *not* taste good. I couldn't even remember a time when I didn't know how to swim. Being in water was so essential to Louis, Charlie, and me that our lives would've been completely different if we didn't have regular access to the lake. Diving into the water, fishing, and canoeing were where we had most of my memories during childhood. Everything the three of us did seemed to revolve around water. "Are you interested in learning how? I could teach you."

"I think I'm a little too old to learn now." A cynical laugh leaked out of her, and I already missed the sound of her happy giggling.

"It would just be another first that I could be there for." I reached for her hand that was curled into her chest and pried it away to be held by me linking our thumbs in our signature hand-holding grasp.

After a long exhale, she nodded. "Okay. But maybe not today? I really feel like I want to rest for a little while."

"I can stay with you while you rest." I still wasn't one hundred percent sure she was okay after running into her father, so I wanted to stay close by if she needed me.

"I'm really just going to take a nap." Her eyelids began to look heavy on her. "Just tell me what time to be ready for dinner. You're going to pick me up, right?"

"Yes. Of course." I was reluctant to leave her alone, but I certainly didn't want to impose when she made it very clear that she still wanted to see me later. "I can go if you want to rest." I began to sit upright, while her head remained on her pillow. "I may go to the gym and then run home to get ready before coming back over. What time is it okay for me to come back?"

"Anytime this afternoon is fine with me." Fatigue trickled throughout her speech.

"Okay, but you don't like for me to show up unannounced, so maybe you should give me a time to come over?" After the comment left my mouth, the most unexpected thing happened. She sat up next to me and gently pecked my lips with hers. It was over quickly, but the softness from her touch left a tingling on my mouth.

"Just let me sleep for a couple of hours, and then show up whenever you like." A wave of emotion began to roll through me. I had never felt this way about anyone ever in my life. I couldn't wait to see her, to hold her, to be with her again, and I hadn't even left her side yet. She already held a piece of my heart in her hand. I just needed to learn how to capture a piece of hers.

After my much-needed workout, I decided to text my mom and give her a heads-up about a few things prior to dinner.

Cam: Please DON'T ask anything about Lex's parents today.

Mommarita: Okay. I won't.

Cam: I'm serious Mommarita. I don't want you to upset my girlfriend.

Mommarita: Your girlfriend? I thought you said you were just friends getting to know each other.

Cam: Yeah, well things have changed.

Mommarita: [the cast of Friends jumping up and down with excitement GIF] I was certain you would win her over.

Cam: Don't get ahead of yourself.

Mommarita: Okay. I won't. [smiley face, smiley face]

I really hoped my mom wouldn't screw things up for me with Lex. Sure, she would welcome her with open arms, but I just hoped she didn't push my new girlfriend too hard. I had never brought a girl home before. I was twenty-three and should've had many opportunities to introduce a love interest to my mother before, but I had absolutely no interest in love prior to Alexis. The only girls who ever came to my parents' house were the few who were bold enough to sneak into my bedroom when I was in high school.

It was natural for Louis to be at their house. He was like my brother for my whole childhood, so it was an easy transition for Charlie. She'd had a few relationships that lasted for more than a few months in high school and college, but she didn't bring anyone home, either. Having Louis come along for a family dinner now wasn't any big deal because he was a regular previously. No one made a big deal over the fact that my twin brought her boyfriend home.

However, when I decided to bring over a significant other, I imagined there would be an ovation and celebration. Claudette, on the other hand, invited boys over for family dinners all the time. I swear she would meet someone and have him over that evening to meet our parents. She had never been serious about anyone, but she wanted to fall in love. Nonetheless, the overwhelming need for her to have my parents' approval was disturbing. It was almost like she brought every guy over right away to see how our parents would react to him. I had no idea if she ever fell in love or not. She moved away a few years ago, so family dinners with her present essentially stopped for a long period of time.

Unfortunately, I must admit that I didn't really feel like I knew my oldest sibling very well anymore. We were never close. Charlie was my favorite sister for sure, but I at least used to have interactions with Claudette. Now, I barely spoke to her. Louis left my life for five years, and I didn't realize how much that sucked until I had him back home again. Therefore, since Claudette recently moved back, I decided to make more of an effort to get to know her again. It was a little weird that she'd asked Travis to come to dinner and told Mom he was my friend. I guess she wasn't worried about what kind of impression he would make with my parents. Or maybe she didn't want to admit she liked him in case my parents didn't.

I loved my parents, but I certainly couldn't care less if they liked Lex or not. She was my girlfriend, and they would have to accept that regardless. *Who am I kidding?* My mom would absolutely love her. She'd freak out and talk to Lex about wedding planning. I was in so much trouble.

I tried my best to warn Lex that she may be hugged. She doesn't particularly like to be held. I hoped to change that, but for now, I would do my best to warn her that my mom could come off a little strong in the smothering embraces department. I was right to warn her.

My mom greeted us at the door. No one else had arrived yet, so all attention was on us. My mom kissed me on the cheek and gave me a quick squeeze. My dad pulled me into a brief man-hug, but still managed to give me a peck on my forehead. What can I say? We were a touchy-feely kind of family.

My dad at least made his hug with Lex short-lived. My mom, however, not only held her longer and tighter than was probably appropriate for meeting someone for the first time, but she actually squealed. My mom screeched and squawked like a kid getting a favorite toy on Christmas morning.

My mom reminded me of my sisters. Most of the time, she was a badass attorney who reminded me of Claudette. She was no-nonsense, grace, and beauty. But when she squeaked with delight, I could see Charlie in her, for sure. Charlie used to get teased when we were younger about the screeching she would do when she was happy.

Of course, being around Louis and me most of the time, girly squealing didn't happen from either of us. But when she scored a goal in field hockey or won a race in track, Charlie screeched louder than any other girl.

"It's nice to meet you, Mr. and Mrs.…"

My mom visibly cringed, and Lex slapped her hand across her mouth.

"Just call us Rita and John, sweetheart." My mom smiled reassuringly at Lex, urging her to uncover her lips.

Thankfully, Charlie and Louis entered the house at that moment. My dad hugged everyone and kissed each of them on their foreheads. He'd been showing affection to all three of us for so long it didn't seem weird to any of us, but I wondered what Lex must think about a grown man kissing the foreheads of grown children, both male and female.

My dad stood the same height as me, and I was fortunate enough to inherit his hazel eyes. It was definitely my most striking feature. My mom had the same petite build and wavy dirty-blond hair as Claudette, and the same gray eyes as Charlie.

My dad didn't just show his affection to the ones he considered his children, but he directed his unconditional to my mom as well. They were extremely affectionate with each other. Truly, it was probably what Claudette was always chasing, and what Charlie and I never thought possible. But now, when I saw my two best friends interact with each other, I believed it was possible for others, too.

Louis and Charlie were completely at ease with each other. They exchanged inside jokes and adorning glances. It was true that I sometimes acted like I was repulsed at their public displays of affection, but it was really just a cover for my envy. Granted, I'd had my share of affection from females. I had always enjoyed that, but now I was at a point in my life where I wanted something more. I didn't think having a meaningful relationship was in the cards for me until now.

I recognized early on that Lex was different from other girls. For one thing, she didn't go for my usual charm. She was initially quiet and standoffish. I'd had to peel away those outer layers of her timidity, but being able to bring her out of her shell had been a very rewarding experience. Now that I understood why I always had such a magnetic pull toward her, I didn't plan on ever letting her go.

"Cameron, go get yourself and Alexis some drinks while your dad and I finish getting the appetizers ready," my mother said while shooing us with her wildly waving hands.

"My mom really went all out. We don't usually have appetizers. It must be because I brought a guest." I reached for Lex's hand and ushered her into the kitchen for our beverages.

While in the kitchen, I heard the front door sweep open and Louis say, "Hey, Claude." However, I didn't hear any additional voices. I had assumed Travis was coming with her. My parents' house was not the open concept design that modern homes had within their first-floor plan. Lex and I were in the kitchen grabbing wine from the fridge with a wall separating our view into the living room and foyer area.

When I emerged with Lex at my side and a wineglass for her and a bottle of beer for me, I saw that what I had suspected was true. "Where's Travis?" I asked my oldest sibling.

She darted a death stare in my direction. "I assume he'll be here soon." Her expression transformed into a scowl, and I wasn't sure why. "What time did you tell him to be here?"

I always had a pretty good idea of what went through Charlie's head. She was my twin, after all, but for some reason, I now had an idea of what was going through Claudette's. Maybe I was just getting better at reading women in general. What I didn't understand was that if this was my big sister's plan, why didn't she inform me beforehand so I could at least act like I had a clue?

"I told him to just come over after golf." She better show some gratitude, at least. Even I was impressed at how quickly I came up with that recovery. I still wasn't sure what was going on between my sister and Travis, but I also knew if she was going to confide in a sibling, it wouldn't be me. It would be Charlie. "Maybe I should text him."

"No." Claudette almost grabbed my phone out of my

pocket before I could even reach for it. "If he's at the golf course, he won't be able to respond. I'm sure he'll be here soon."

Claudette's panic-ridden voice concerned me, so I turned to face my girlfriend. "Hey, Lex, will it be okay with you if I leave you with Louis and Charlie for just a minute? I need to talk with Claude." I needed to get to the bottom of this. She flashed me a sweet smile, and I released her hand so she could join Charlie and Louis. Then I motioned my head toward Claudette in the direction of the kitchen.

"What the hell is going on, Claude?" I whispered once behind the kitchen wall to avoid our parents overhearing our conversation. They were tucked away in the formal dining room presumably setting out appetizers.

"I didn't tell Mom and Dad that I had invited Travis." She glared at me with burning, reproachful eyes. *What the hell have I done?*

"Okay, so what's the plan?" Even though she appeared madder than hell, I still wanted to find out what she expected to happen.

"I told Mom that Travis was your friend. I had no idea you were going to invite a girl over." She spoke softly also, but she over-enunciated her words. Basically, her voice was a screaming whisper.

"Her name is Alexis, and you've met her before. She went to dinner with us." I wore a perplexed expression because *what did having Alexis over have anything to do with Travis?*

"I know what her name is, you idiot. I meant that you have *never* brought a girl home, so why would I assume you were bringing *any* girl?" Her eyebrows were furrowed, and although we hadn't always gotten along, I had never been a bad brother to her. I had no idea what all the hostility was about.

"What difference does it make if I bring someone over or not?"

She really needed to be more direct. *What happened to the no-nonsense approach she usually had?*

"Now that Charlie is with Louis and you are with Alexis, it's going to look like I'm with Travis." At this point, she had her jaw clenched so tightly that her whispers practically shot through the tiny spaces between her teeth.

"So?" It wasn't like she hadn't brought a hundred boys over for family dinners before.

"So? Travis will think I planned this whole thing so I could get paired with him." Her blue eyes began to glass over, as if tears caused them to shine. I really, really hoped she didn't cry.

"First of all, I don't think Travis will suspect that you manipulated him into coming to dinner as a love interest. And secondly, why didn't you at least text or call me to give me a heads-up?"

Her facial features were turned downward, and the usually flawless skin across her face was splattered with red splotches. I was not used to seeing her upset, but I moved toward her and rubbed her shoulders in response to whatever was unfolding between us. I was not the type to be comfortable around an emotional woman, but I felt like I needed to reassure her somehow.

"I get that I'm not your favorite sibling, but I'll always have your back."

Holy crap. I saw a smile creep across her face. She actually smiled because of something I said. "Cammy, you have never seemed interested in helping me, hanging out with me, or even learning anything about me."

"Probably because you call me Cammy." We both exchanged a few, brief laughs. "Listen, I can play along with whatever charade you're up for, but really, next time, you need to tell me about it."

"I guess it's not too late for you to be my favorite sibling." Wow. She was an easy sell.

"You have no loyalty. But I love you anyway." I hugged her but had to murmur under my breath, "Sorry, Claude. The title of my favorite sibling will always belong to Lean Bean."

"Oh, I know." She abruptly pulled out of my embrace and shot me a cold look. "You, Charlie, and Louis have always had each other. I don't have that close-knit group of people. And now with Charlie and Alexis becoming friends, my own sister won't have any time for me. I always counted on being the female presence in Char's life. She never had female friends before, but she had me. Now that she has a girlfriend, where does that leave me?"

"What the hell are you talking about? Who did she run to when she and Louis had their blow-out fight? It certainly wasn't me! She wanted her sister. And what do you mean, you don't have a close-knit group of people? You've always had plenty of friends. I figured you were all still close." It was beginning to sound like Claudette was having a quarter-life crisis. Maybe she and I actually did have a few similarities after all.

"Well, you figured wrong! They're all busy getting married. Sure, I've been a bridesmaid a dozen times, but I'm not getting married anytime soon. Some of them are already talking about babies! I don't have anything in common with them anymore." She heaved a deep sigh and grabbed the back of her neck. "Travis has been a good friend to me. He's going through some stuff, and although my drama isn't nearly at the same magnitude, he understands me." She reached for my hand. "So can you just play along? I don't want to put any pressure on Travis, and I definitely don't want Mom and Dad to think he's my boyfriend. They'll never in a million years believe that I'm only friends with a man, so it would just be easier if we tell them that you and Charlie are friends with him."

"All right. It's fine, really." I changed the way she held my hand into a handshake just as our mother rounded the corner to witness our very weird agreement.

"John, you've got to see this," my mom said while taking a platter to the sink.

My dad appeared in the open doorway that separated the kitchen from the dining area. "What's that?"

"Our oldest and our youngest look like they're getting along. Should we be worried?" My mother arched an eyebrow in our direction.

"It definitely looks like a conspiracy." My father chuckled and swatted my mother on her behind. She flinched and laughed back at him. Claude and I exchanged glances and then simultaneously made upchucking noises.

Dinner went well. Once Travis finally showed up, I effectively convinced my parents that he was my friend...and of course, Charlie's, too. It was true that we were all friends, but the whole situation was bizarre. It felt normal to have Louis at my parents' house, but with him as Charlie's boyfriend and not our childhood pal was definitely different. Bringing a girl to my parents' house felt odd too, but at the same time, I couldn't imagine having anyone else as my girlfriend other than Lex. That was really peculiar. First of all, calling *anyone* my girlfriend should be strange enough, but feeling like Lex was the only woman who would ever have that title should feel weird, right?

My mother couldn't stop smiling the whole time we were there. When I was clearing the table with her as the others were doing the dishes, she whispered in my ear, "Cameron, there is nothing that makes a mother happier than seeing her children so happy." I definitely was happy with Lex. I was happier than I had ever been with another human being. I was sure she enjoyed seeing both of her twins happy, with the Charlie-Louis show and all, too. With Louis being like a second son to her, maybe she included him in the category of "her children." I wondered what she thought of Claudette's situation.

My oldest sister had recently moved in with my parents after living an hour away in a Delaware beach town for several years. She attended college, and immediately following her undergraduate degree, she pursued an MBA. Rather than work in the corporate world as Charlie and I assumed she would, she decided to work retail after grad school and managed a coffee shop for the last five years.

When her boss decided to open a new shop in our hometown, she very happily accepted the position to open and manage the new store. Rather than rent an apartment, she moved back into our parents' house during that transition time. One might see a twenty-five-year-old moving back in with Mom and Dad as an admission of failure, but Claudette saw it as an in-between residence while she decided on returning to Sandy Cove for good or going back to her Delaware beach town once the new store was up and doing well. The owner was letting her decide which store she wanted to make her permanent employment.

Claudette and Travis had had some interesting interactions that evening. She actually treated him like a friend—if that was even possible. I didn't witness any giggling or the tossing of her blond hair that she was famous for when she spoke to him. She didn't stare into his eyes like he was the only person in the world, but rather they talked about whatever random topic came up with ease. It was the other weird thing about the evening. I wondered if Claudette seeming content and relaxed was also part of my mom being delighted about seeing her children happy.

❦

"So am I staying at your place tonight? Or do you want to stay at mine?" I asked Lex while leaving my parents' house.

"I don't think we need to spend every night together, Cam." Her focus remained on the road ahead, even though I was the one driving.

"Well, of course not. You work three nights a week." I assumed now that we had a title and relationship status, it meant we would be sleeping together. *Besides, what if she has another nightmare?* I needed to be there for her.

"I'm having a hard time trying to adjust to all the changes going on in my life at the moment." Her apprehension was apparent as she shifted uncomfortably in her seat.

"Lex, the last thing I want to do is upset you. If you don't want me to spend the night, I will respect that. I have to go to work early in the morning, so I can just go back to my apartment. Those field hockey and soccer players like to practice at six forty-five." I really did want to respect her alone time, but I felt like it was going to slowly squeeze the living breath out of me.

"So if you stay at mine, you'll need to get up even earlier to run back to your apartment and get ready for work?" She finally turned toward me and leaned the side of her head against the leather interior of my truck. *Did she not understand that I would go without sleep just to spend more time with her?*

"Yes. I suppose that's true." I tried to keep my eyes on the road, but she looked so beautiful with her light brown hair splayed across the back of my truck's seat.

"Then I suppose I should stay at your place." *Did those words actually come out of her mouth?* She made the statement so matter-of-factly I wasn't sure how to react.

Of course I would try to play it cool. I would desperately try to hide the fact that inside, I was jumping up and down with excitement, just like the GIF my mother had sent me recently. "Okay. Do you want to stop by your apartment to get anything?"

"Yeah, just drop me off and I'll come by in a little bit."

I wasn't sure if this was a good idea or not. She might change her mind and not show. Then again, I could use the extra time to straighten my home up some, maybe change my sheets and make my bed.

"I can wait while you grab your things, and then we could go over together." The sheets weren't *that* dirty.

"Nah. You don't have to do that. I want to drive myself so I have my car tomorrow when you go to work." She reached over and brushed her hand against my thigh.

A sudden rush of warmth shot through my entire body from just her palm touching my leg. I swallowed and continued an attempt at staying focused on driving.

"I have to work tomorrow night, so I'll most likely need to go back home before you come back after work." So she was a practical one. That realization brought a smile across my face. She was sweet and innocent…and practical. My heart turned to mush.

"Do you always think everything out?" I glanced away from the road for just one second to peer in her direction. "Haven't you ever just done something spontaneous? Like… something impulsive."

"Cam, I am able to live in the moment, if that's what you mean. But I do believe in anticipating what's to come." Damn, she was sexy and didn't even know it. My pants became tight just thinking about *what's to come.*

After a few more minutes of driving, I dropped Lex off at her apartment with just a brief peck on the lips. I wanted to walk her to the door, but being on the first floor, she reminded me that I could actually see her apartment door from the parking lot. I got the feeling that she didn't want me to walk her up. I was still trying to figure her out. I didn't mind, though. I had the rest of my life to learn everything about her.

9
ALEXIS

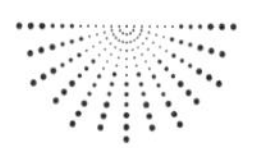

I had no idea what I was doing. I had a boyfriend. I was going to spend the night at his apartment. I wasn't sure what to pack. I didn't know what to do about any of this. There were so many things about me that Cam hadn't discovered. And there were some things that I didn't ever want him to find out. Then there were some things that I guess I probably should share with him. I really had never thought about how many secrets I actually harbored.

He was sweet and patient, and I never would've imagined I'd end up here—with Cam as my boyfriend. I tried so hard to avoid him when he'd come into the ER to visit Charlie. I actually found the swagger in his step and the blatant flirting repulsive. Tiffany and Cecilia liked it too much, and I just didn't see it. I mistook his confidence as cockiness.

But some part of me felt as if I had been waiting my whole life for him. That little girl on the bus loved him. She needed him, and he was there for her. I remembered trusting him back then. *So why am I having such a hard time trusting him now?* Sure, times had changed. I had seen way more shit now than that little girl had at five years old. But had he changed, too? He seemed very much like he wanted to resume his Batman status and distract me from my issues. He had been kind and understanding. I wasn't sure I deserved him. He had made it clear that he was interested in hearing about my secrets, but I didn't want to reveal everything to him. It just wasn't going to happen.

I was still caught up in my thoughts when I pulled into Cam's apartment complex. After hoisting my overnight bag over my shoulder, I took in a huge breath and walked one foot in front of the other up the stairs to his apartment. The door was slightly ajar when I approached.

"Cam…" I searched the living room but didn't see him. I pried the door open further so I could enter. "Cam…" I stated again while shutting the door behind me. I tossed my bag on the floor and cautiously began walking down the short hallway. His bedroom door was open, so I peered inside.

He was actively shaking a pillow into a pillowcase when I repeated, "Cam."

He turned in my direction, quickly dropping said pillow onto his bed. "Hey, Butterfly." He approached me with a quick kiss on the lips, and my pulse increased in rate and intensity. "Sorry. I didn't think I'd hear you knock, so I left the door open. But then I didn't hear you come in." He reached into his pocket as he added, "I have something for you."

I looked at his hand emerging from the front pocket of his jeans and saw a copper-colored key emerge.

He regarded me quizzically for a moment. Obviously, he saw the shock written across my face. I was certain my cheeks turned white because I felt the color drain from my head and neck. I opened my mouth to speak, but I was at a loss for words. He ignored my wary reaction and reached for my hand, nonetheless. Then he placed the piece of metal into my palm, closing my fingers around it.

"Don't look so devastated. It's so you can come and go whenever you like. You're my girlfriend, so I want you to have a key to my place. I don't expect the key to yours. I just want you to understand that you are always welcome here."

I felt my chin beginning to curl downward to my chest when I felt his finger pull my head upward so my eyes met his.

"Charlie and Louis also have keys…but you are the only woman I've dated that I wanted to give my key to. Charlie and Louis are my two best friends, but now with you back in my life, you aren't just my girlfriend, you're one of my best friends, too. So please, always remember that I'm your friend. I was your friend when we were kids, and I'm your friend now that we are grownups."

"Okay." With a whoosh from the release of the breath I didn't know I had been holding, it was all I could manage to say.

"You will eventually trust me. You may not have completely trusted me when we were kids, but I swear, you can trust me with anything. Always." His finger left my chin and his strong arms wrapped around me. I guess I was getting better at accepting hugs. I stood there with the warmth of Cam pressed against me, and I didn't feel compelled to step back or wiggle myself free from his hold.

Instead, I snaked my arms around his neck and pulled him in to me. *Where did that come from?* "I'm going to try." I really wanted to be able to confide in him. I'd been unnecessarily carrying around a lot of secrets. He hadn't made a big deal about my jerk of a father…well, no more than was essential. He didn't hold it against me. I guess I always feared that I would be shunned and discarded for my background if anyone found out about my past. But this man clearly wanted to be with me regardless of my disastrous childhood. *Could there really be kind, gentle men in the world who are thoughtful and caring?*

He gazed into my eyes while I was lost in my thoughts, so I missed the look on his face that indicated he was about to kiss me. I flinched when I felt his mouth touch mine, and he quickly withdrew, shooting me a questioning look. "You okay?"

My lips quivered in response to his sudden departure. I felt slightly dazed—not only from my previous thoughts, but also from the warmth of his body and the soft caress of his lips, causing a power surge of swirling emotion within my chest. I wasn't sure if I was okay. I wasn't sure if I would ever be okay again. I needed to trust this feeling. It was actually a very good feeling. This closeness between us felt wonderfully perfect.

I decided right then and there that I needed to remember who I was. I was Alexis Armstrong, and I wasn't scared of anything. I could be bold and daring, and I shouldn't worry about what anyone thought of me. Cam stood nearly twelve inches from me, so I had to reach a little ways to pull him back toward me. I grasped his cotton shirt, and he leaned forward.

Then, standing on my toes, I brushed my mouth against his. A small moan escaped from his throat, and he cupped my face with his hands as he deepened our kiss. What started as light brushing and pecking turned into a fury of heavy need. With a minimal amount of urging, I relaxed my jaw to allow him access to explore freely. He devoured my mouth like he was starving to taste me. His tongue was minty. I figured he must've just brushed his teeth because the taste of chicken cacciatore and beer that he'd feasted on at his parents' house was noticeably absent. He smelled of soap and a woodsy fragrance that I decided I was infatuated with. It was a scent that was unique to him. *Had he always smelled so delicious?*

His lips left my mouth and began a trail from my jawline down the hollow of my throat, shifting the neckline of my shirt to give gentle pecks along my collarbone. A strange feeling stirred within my belly. It wasn't a bad, sickly feeling. It was an intensely good, amazing feeling.

"Cam," I huffed out in my near-breathless state because the man really did take my breath away.

"Yes, Butterfly," he said in between his lips' caresses, but never losing focus of the trail he left behind.

"Kiss me on the mouth again, please."

Without any protest, he reconnected his soft, roaming lips to my mouth and nibbled at my bottom lip. My head buzzed with drunken dizziness. I didn't think I had ever been kissed like that. I just knew I never wanted it to stop.

With our mouths still fused in their uncontrolled passion, I slipped my hand beneath his cotton shirt. I just wanted to touch him. I ran my fingers over the hard ridges of his abdomen while our kissing continued, but with a swift motion, Cam broke us apart for only a fraction of a second to pull his shirt over his head and toss it to the floor.

With our mouths once again joined in their ecstasy, I moved my hands from his abdomen to his impressive pecs and then down his biceps and forearms. My God, he was smoking hot! I'd never had an attraction like this to anyone before.

As he brushed his fingertip across my breast, grazing my nipple with his touch, I felt a sensation shoot through me. I literally gasped at the tingling feeling rocking through my core. I had never experienced anything like that before. He stopped our kiss and, again, gave me the *are-you-okay* look. I smiled and nodded emphatically.

He returned his attention back to my nipples and rolled his fingertips across them over the material of my shirt and bra. I guess his imagination of what I looked like beneath my clothes wasn't enough for him. He slid his hand beneath my shirt, and I felt the instant heat of his palm on my belly. *Did the temperature in his apartment just increase by twenty degrees?* The overwhelming need to pull off my shirt whirled through me, so I willingly indulged in that fleeting thought. With a swift pull, I yanked the soft, stretchy material over my head and tossed it on the floor somewhere near Cam's.

His hazel eyes shone with a hunger and desire I hadn't seen him wear before. He commenced with kissing me again, touching the exposed skin of my chest and the top of my breasts. When he sucked at my nipple through the lacy covering of my bra, I knew that last bit of material needed to go. As I struggled to reach behind me with not a coordinated, graceful motion in the least, Cam reached around me and released the clasp of my bra with one efficient, nimble motion. I chose to ignore the fact that he had clearly practiced that move. He had done this before. I pushed that thought away and tried to focus on this one moment in time.

When I shucked the undergarment off my breasts and now stood before him completely exposed from the waist up, he quickly resumed his gentle sucking to my sensitive nipples. I could feel them harden from the wetness of his mouth. The swirling motion he did with his tongue flooded my senses with waves of pleasure, making me dizzy. I mean, *oh my God.*

Cam looked up at me and smiled. *Did I say that out loud?* He didn't let me regain my composure enough to even be embarrassed. I was quickly losing all ability to think. I was losing my ability to stand. And as if my brain transmitted that thought to my lower extremities, my legs felt as if they wouldn't support my weight any longer. But just as I was about to melt into a puddle on his bedroom floor from the Jell-O-like feeling in my lower extremities, he pulled me closer and guided me to his bed.

It was a comfortable bed. But soon, I was writhing beneath him as he sucked one of my nipples into his mouth while rolling the other between his thumb and index finger. "If at any point you don't want this, just say so, and I'll stop."

I heard his words, but was he insane? I didn't *ever* want him to stop. I shifted my hips against his, and I could feel the evidence of his arousal. I briefly wondered how many women had had that effect on him, but that was short-lived. I couldn't think clearly for much more than a moment. He reached for the waistband of my shorts, and I moved to allow him better access so he could more easily unbutton the denim.

I lifted my hips so he could shimmy my shorts and panties down my legs with one swift motion. Kisses across my nipples and down my abdomen followed, and soon, I felt his finger within the swollen folds between my legs. A warm and amazing moistness flowed out of me, coating my lady parts. Cam moaned again. "You're so wet, and it's driving me crazy. Everything about you drives me crazy."

He slipped a finger into me with ease, and once he began to thrust in and out, I was soon matching his movements with my pelvis. He skillfully slipped another finger inside me and began applying pressure with his thumb on a very sensitive nub seated at the top of my swollen folds of flesh. When his tongue swirled my nipples again, a trembling force raked over my body. *Ohmigod. Ohmigod. Ohmigod.*

I thought that was my voice I heard, but considering I was somehow floating above my body at that moment, I wasn't entirely sure. The waves of pleasure continued for several moments, and when the release of what was probably the only orgasm I'd ever had in my life had completely exhausted me, I welcomed the relaxation to take over my body. My eyes closed, and I felt at peace. I felt calm and thoroughly comfortable.

"I wasn't expecting that," I uttered while still basking in the afterglow and keeping my eyes shut.

"Neither was I." He removed his fingers from within me and kissed my swollen lips. "Tell me a secret."

"A secret?" I shook my head and attempted to move out from beneath him. Realizing that I was still uncomfortably naked, I reached for the bedspread to cover my exposed skin.

Seeing my discomfort, Cam grabbed his shirt off the floor and handed it to me. I wasted no time pulling it over my head and tugging it down to cover all my lady parts.

"I don't mean a secret, per se. I just mean, tell me something I don't know. I want to learn everything about you." He linked his thumb with mine. I was beginning to think he realized that gesture held a sweet spot in my heart. That precious memory had replayed in my head over and over again, always giving me a happy outlet. *How can I say no to anything when he makes a butterfly out of holding my hand?* He was probably already aware of this, but if he wasn't, I didn't want him to let on that he could have that kind of power over my actions.

"I like salad, but I don't like salad dressing." It was a meaningless piece of personal information, but I had to offer him something.

He smiled before hugging me, and I swear, he sniffed my hair. "Was that too difficult?"

"Well, you gave me my first orgasm, so I guess I felt like I owed you something." I was kidding, but he pulled away quickly, and those damn hazel eyes bore into my soul.

"First of all, you don't *ever* owe me anything. Got it?"

I nodded silently.

"And secondly…*really*? That was your *first*?" I nodded again, and the smile that stretched across his gorgeous face revealed the devilish grin that I always thought was trouble. "Well, I said I wanted to be there for all your firsts." Then his lips met mine again.

I went into the bathroom to brush my teeth and change into the pajamas I had packed. When I walked back into Cam's room, he was lying beneath the covers. The bedspread was covering part of him, but his very exposed, shirtless chest was on display. *Is he planning to sleep without his shirt?*

He patted the spot next to him. I tentatively approached and sat next to him, sinking into the mattress.

"Aren't you going to get under the covers?" His hand brushed alongside my thigh, and I was glad I had on long pants instead of shorts.

"This feels weird to me." I was about to sleep with a man. Not have sex with a man. I had never done that before. And I didn't feel ready to do that with Cam. "Tell me something about you." Maybe if he shared more things about himself, it wouldn't feel so awkward.

Cam sat up straighter so the quilt fell further down his body. Now, not only his chest, but his chiseled abs were on display as well. "What do you want to know? I told you, I'll reveal any secret you want to hear."

"It doesn't need to be a secret." I glanced at him, then at his bed, and around his room, painfully feeling out of place.

"Are you wondering how many other girls have slept here?" Damn, he was perceptive. "The answer is none. I'm sure you aren't interested in hearing specifics about my previous relationships, but you are curious if I have ever slept next to another woman." He grabbed my hand and pulled me toward him with enough force that I almost fell right on top of him. I managed to catch myself with my other hand by resting it on his chest. "Butterfly, you are the only woman I want to have next to me while I sleep. I want to see you right before I close my eyes for the night, and I want to see you first thing in the morning when they open for the first time of the day." Well damn. "So please, crawl under these covers so I can go to sleep holding you."

I couldn't very well say no. I mean, I was already in my pajamas. So I slipped beneath the blanket and curled onto my side. Cam pulled me close and effectively spooned me. He kissed the back of my neck, which sent a wonderful shiver down my spine. "Goodnight, Butterfly."

I didn't have any nightmares that night. In fact, I slept so well that when I woke up the next day, I was in near panic mode; I opened my eyes and didn't recognize where I was. It quickly brought me back to my homeless days. It was dangerous to fall asleep anywhere, really. I'd become so accustomed to only closing my eyelids for very brief periods of time and retaining a light sleeper status when I did succumb to slumber. Although, even with my eyes closed, I still felt very aware of the environment around me.

So after the wave of terror passed through me, I realized I was in Cam's room. I could still smell him next to me, but he wasn't there. The room was bright from the sunlight of the day bouncing off the walls, shining in through the cracks of the mini-blinds covering his windows.

I reluctantly pulled back the comforter and sheet to release my legs and swung them around to the side of the bed so I could drop my feet onto the carpet. It was quiet in his apartment. I was sure he wasn't there. I would have sensed him. I peered into the bathroom and walked into the living room and kitchen area. He wasn't there, either.

There was a note folded in half and taped to the door. There was a butterfly drawn on the front of the paper. When I approached it, I realized it wasn't just a drawing. It was a sketch with shading and details that had obviously taken a long time to complete. It was done in plain pencil, but I was impressed with the delicate features captured on the piece of paper.

Knowing he had drawn this beautiful piece of art for me made me want to cry. Not sad tears, but happy ones. The joyous kind that developed with a surge of emotion in your chest, moved up your throat, made you smile, and formed into water leaking from the corners of your eyes.

Butterfly,

You were sleeping so peacefully when I woke up that I didn't want to wake you. I was hoping you were having good dreams. I had to go to work, but we can talk later. I'm pretty sure you have ruined me from ever being able to sleep in my bed without you now. I don't think I've ever slept so soundly in my life. I love feeling the warmth of your body cuddled up next to me, and your easy breathing is a very calming sound. Charlie told me you work the next few nights. I'll be by with coffee. I miss you already, and I haven't even left yet.

C-

The little heart next to the capital letter C made that emotional wave return through my body. This was crazy. He made my legs turn to Jell-O, ignited a fire of desire within me, and warmed my heart with how sweet he was. I wasn't doing a very good job of not falling for him. I was falling hard. I would just have to keep telling the doubtful part of me that he was a good person, and I could trust him.

Alexis: I need to talk to you. You working tonight?

Charlie: Yep. But you can call if you want.

Alexis: I would rather speak in person if that's all right.

Charlie: Yep. No problem. See you then.

I really needed to tell someone how I was feeling. It was so wonderful that I wanted to share it with someone. This was still foreign territory to me. I had grown so accustomed to being alone that having people to go to for advice or share exciting news was a new concept, but surprisingly, marvelous. I wondered if this reaction was what happened to a middle school girl when she wanted to tell her best girlfriend about the boy she was crushing on. I missed out on those times, so maybe I was playing catch up on a lot of things now. Cam said I still had a lot of firsts. I guess blurting out my feelings for a man to my best girlfriend was one of those firsts, even if my best girlfriend happened to be his twin sister.

Regardless of her relation to Cam, I was hopeful she would be supportive and encouraging. After all, her boyfriend was her twin brother's best friend. Granted, their situation was a little different. Charlie and Louis had been friends since forever—well, minus that five-year hiatus. They'd grown up together. Even though Cam and I had known each other a long time ago, we hadn't spent our childhood together. Oh, and our hiatus was a decade longer.

Cam was right. Waking up from my nap in bed that afternoon wasn't nearly as good as waking up with the smell of him next to me. I missed him. I had a good idea he would bring me coffee that night, so I decided to send him a text about something I was pretty sure he was clueless about.

Alexis: I probably should have told you this earlier, but there is something you need to know about me.

Cam: ???

Alexis: I don't really like coffee.

Cam: [shocked face emoji]

Alexis: I prefer hot chocolate.

Cam: Why didn't you say anything before now? I feel terrible bringing you something you didn't want all this time.

I had to think for a moment about how to respond. I had told myself that I wouldn't be afraid. I wanted to be bold and daring.

Alexis: Maybe it was the guy bringing me the coffee that I wanted.

Cam: You're awful brazen in a text message. Say it to my face next time.

Alexis: I can't wait.

Cam: Neither can I :-)

Sure, I was innocent with certain things. But no one could ever accuse me of being naïve. With a smile on my face, I walked into the emergency room and headed straight for the locker room. I found Charlie grabbing her stethoscope out of her metal cabinet as I entered the small, quiet room.

"Just so you know, it's not cool to make your friend wait all day before dishing out the gossip." Charlie slammed her locker door shut with a loud thump, but she wore an animated smile. "So spill!"

"I really like your brother." Maybe I should've said the words differently, but I honestly didn't think before they came spilling out.

Her smile widened, if that was even possible. "This is the best news I've heard in a long time." She approached me quickly—too fast for me to take a step back before she practically smothered me in an embrace. I'd been dodging hugs my whole life, but it seemed like Charlie, Cam, and their family had hugged me more in the last few weeks than all the times throughout my life that I tried to avert them put together.

I didn't pull away from her. Maybe I was getting more comfortable with embraces from them.

She pushed away a moment later to speak. "My best girlfriend and my brother." And then she squeezed the heck out of me for another ridiculous embrace. I just stood there with my arms pinned to my sides while my crazy friend rested her chin on my shoulder with her arms wrapped around me. "This must be how Ross felt when he found out about Monica and Chandler." She was still hugging me when she referenced the nineties sitcom.

She pushed away from me again and placed her hand on her hip. I had seen a similar stance from her when she was annoyed. "But seriously, you couldn't have told me that over the phone? Or in a text?"

"This is going to sound stupid, but I was excited to tell you my exciting news…in person." My confession *did* sound stupid. "I wanted to see your reaction."

"Well, as I'm sure I have already told you, he really likes you, too. And now that you two are together, it will make Cam feel less awkward around Louis and me. He was never a third wheel before, but since Louis and I have been *more than friends*, I guess he feels like he is sometimes. We try not to make it weird, but I guess sometimes it is." Charlie began braiding her light brown hair, so she turned to look in the mirror hanging on the wall next to the lockers.

We still had fifteen minutes before our shift started, and there was no one else in the locker room at the time, so I had another confession to make. "Your brother and I have slept together, but we haven't *slept* together." I watched her face twitch in the mirror, even though she had her back to me at that moment. "I've never done that with anyone before."

After my admitted remark, Charlie dropped her braid and quickly turned on her heel to face me. "You've never had sex before?" Then she lowered her voice, recognizing that it may have been inappropriate to blurt that out. "You're a virgin?" The volume of her tone dropped several more decibels to barely a whisper.

I mimicked her whispered voice. "Virgin isn't a bad word."

"I know it's not. It's just private, and I felt bad about saying it so loudly, even if it's just you and me in here." Her voice rose slightly, but she still whispered.

"Well then, you are really going to want to speak softly for a while longer. I'm thinking about your brother being my first." I continued to whisper my plan only to tease my friend.

She visibly shuttered. "And now I guess this is how Cameron felt when I talked to him about sex with Louis." She smacked her forehead with an open palm, just like the emoji.

"You didn't!" The harshness and intensity of my voice increased in volume.

She dropped her open palm and clasped her hands behind her neck at that point. "I needed to talk to someone. I had already gone to my sister, and I didn't feel any better, so I had to talk to my best friend. It just so happens that my brother is my best friend, but he is also the best friend of the man I had sex with."

If I wasn't completely aware of Cam, Charlie, and Louis's story, I would have been completely confused by her last statement. The way everything was so intertwined would've been hard for an outsider to try to keep track of. "I'm sorry if this is weird for you. But I like having a friend I can talk to. It's not something I ever thought I wanted or needed, but now that I have it, I kind of like it."

Charlie sighed deeply and returned to the mirror so she could redo her braid. "Well, okay. But no specifics, please. He *is* my brother." Obviously not liking the braid she completed, she returned to her locker to fetch a hairbrush and began to brush her hair with long strokes. "So, I can't even believe I'm going to ask you this but…have you thought of when this might happen?"

"Maybe this weekend?" I worked the next three nights in a row, but I had Thursday, Friday, and Saturday off. I gulped down the awkwardness that was building in my throat before I spoke again. "Could you maybe go shopping with me?"

She swung her head around, causing her hair to fan out. If she had finishing redoing her braid, it probably would have smacked her in the face after the whiplash she had just given herself. "Do you mean for, like, sexy underwear and stuff?" Her eyes gave me the impression that she was both a little shocked and a little curious.

"Yeah, I guess."

And then she planted her palm against her forehead again. "Karma's a bitch." She sighed deeply, looking upward to the ceiling. "This must be my punishment for talking to Cameron about sex with Louis."

"If it's too uncomfortable for you, it's no big deal. I can—"

She dropped her head and held up her hand to stop me mid-sentence.

"I'll go shopping with you. Louis would probably appreciate it if I bought something for myself, too." For a second, I thought she was about to hug me again, but with the hairbrush still in her hand, she grabbed both of my shoulders and looked me square in the eyes. "I'm not used to having girlfriends, but I'm sure that if my bestie is going to give up her V-card, then I should go shopping for sexy lingerie with her. So I'll be there for you…doing what any bestie would do."

A satisfied smile pulled at my face while she once again returned to attempting to braid her hair. I really liked having Charlie as a friend. I wondered what would happen if Cam and I stopped dating. I tried to push that thought out of my mind. He promised that we would always be friends. So hopefully, even if we weren't romantically together, we would still be friends. I'd held no dreams about my future beyond completing school and establishing a career. In my younger days, I was always the type who otherwise lived for the moment. I guess I was forced to. *Who could think ahead when you were just trying to survive?* But for some reason, with the Callahans as friends, I could now see a future. I might even let myself dream a little.

Charlie and I worked together Monday and Tuesday night, so I was able to see Cam both nights. He usually only showed up once a week to deliver coffee to his sister and her nursing colleagues, but he showed up twice this week with hot chocolate occupying one of the pockets of the cardboard carrier.

I was able to sneak some amazing kisses from him both nights also. There was an alcove behind the triage area that held random paper documentation for the rare occasion the computer charting system shut down. There were also office supplies, like pens and copier toner. The area was as small as the smallest closet you could envision, but the two of us fit perfectly in the area for a quick kissing session.

Cam and I shared several texts on Wednesday, which included spending the night with each other on Thursday. Charlie and I went shopping Thursday afternoon. I picked out three pairs of lacy panties and a thong with matching bras, while my bestie offered me advice on my selections. She also invited me to sing karaoke with her, Cam, and Louis on Friday night. We were both off on Friday, but she was scheduled to work again Saturday night.

When I returned home from my shopping trip with Charlie, I changed into the lavender bra and panties set I had purchased. Then I switched into a low-cut T-shirt that I was pretty sure Cam liked and a denim skirt before packing an overnight bag and heading over to his apartment.

10
CAMERON

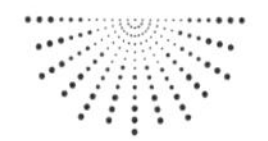

I wasn't sure if I'd be able to resist ripping Lex's clothes off when she got to my apartment. The teasing kisses two nights this week were not enough to kill the semi-hard-on I'd been sporting the last few days. Instead of the mesh shorts I usually wore to work, I had to wear khakis or jeans to hide it. I even tried to relieve myself with my own hand, but my semi-boner just wouldn't settle down completely.

Luckily, the pizza delivery guy didn't notice, or he would've thought I was a pervert. I only slightly opened the door and practically tossed money at him while snatching the box out of his hands. I decided to return to wearing gym shorts that evening. The strain against the tighter fitting garments had become incredibly uncomfortable that week. I hoped I could show some patience and respectfulness when she showed up. I kept telling myself not to maul her as soon as I saw her. In fact, I kept telling myself that up until the time I heard a soft knock at my apartment door.

I didn't even look through the peephole. I knew it was her. I could sense her presence, even on the other side of the heavy metal object. So I swung it open without any shyness of the semi-erection tenting my shorts as it became a full hard-on.

"Hey," she said sweetly as I pulled the door open. Her voice was soft and laced with the temptation of a sugary snack. The self-control I had been grasping onto was completely, utterly gone. I yanked her into the living room, slamming the door behind her.

A split second later, my mouth was on hers, desperate to taste her. She only gasped for a moment and then melted against me, snaking her arms around my neck and kissing me back with as much enthusiasm as I had.

"I gave you a key. You don't have to knock," I muttered while our lips remained melded together.

"I didn't want to startle you." The sound of her voice was muffled from my tongue inside her mouth.

"You might not like surprises, but I freaking love them. Especially if the surprise is you." I kept consuming her with a hunger I hadn't felt since I was a horny teenager. I wasn't sure how much longer I could hold out without an explosion happening in my shorts.

Still fused at the mouth with passionate kissing, I lifted my feet and shuffled them in the direction down the hall toward my room, guiding her along with me. Once we crossed the threshold of my bedroom, my lips left her mouth to show attention to her neck and her collarbone. I slipped my hand along the bottom of her cotton shirt and caressed the smooth skin across her abdomen. She quickly pulled the garment over her head and stood before me in her bra.

Her hair was tousled, and her lips were swollen. I guess I had my fingers in her hair at some point, and I was uncontrollably giving her some bruising kisses. But my God, she was beautiful. She was the prettiest woman I had ever seen, and it wasn't just my erection talking. I wanted to worship her.

I slowed my frantic affection and gently pecked her belly with my lips, moving up her body, eventually letting my tongue roll across the skin of her collarbone. She whimpered quiet moans, which I seriously thought were the sexiest sounds I had ever heard. While still showering her with light pecks, I reached around her and unclasped her bra. Her breasts were released, and I pulled her with me down to my bed.

The aching in my shorts throbbed, but I reminded myself that I needed to hold off addressing my needs. I wanted to make her feel special and provide her unbelievable sensations first. I freaking loved everything about her body, and I wanted to show her my appreciation. I commenced the gratitude I held for her by showing adoration to her breasts. I swirled my tongue around the sensitive peaks and squeezed them between my thumb and index finger because I knew how much she liked that.

I loved that she was wearing a skirt because I could reach up beneath it and have ready access to her warm folds that were swollen with desire. Pushing her panties to the side, I slid my finger into her tight channel. She arched her back and wiggled beneath me. More of those sexy mewls escaped from deep in her throat, so her body was responding favorably. But that wasn't enough. I needed to give her explosion after explosion of pleasure. So I withdrew my finger and resumed kissing her abdomen while I unbuttoned her skirt and pushed it down along with her underwear.

She pulled at my T-shirt while I removed her clothing from the waist down. I readily whisked my shirt over my head while she tickled along my chest with her fingers. I continued the trail of kisses down her abdomen and forged onto her inner thighs. She pulled at my hair, no longer able to reach my chest, since I had traveled too far down her body.

The temptation was too great, with her most sensitive nub now right in front of me. So I let my tongue slide over it. She responded with a flinch but let out a loud moan at the same time. I took that as a sign that she enjoyed it. So I let myself have more of a taste. When I provided the lightest of suction, she screamed my name. I inserted one finger and then two as I continued my focus on her tantalizing, and now engorged, fleshy piece of tissue. She bucked against my mouth, but I held on while she rode out her orgasm. She even begged, pleaded, and shouted, *"don't let go"* as if I had that intention. Witnessing her fall apart right before me was the biggest turn-on I had ever experienced.

When her body fell limp, I removed my mouth from her and trailed kisses back up her abdomen, through her cleavage, and ascended up her neck back to her mouth. She didn't seem reluctant to taste herself on my lips, which I thought was hotter than hell.

With my attention still retained on her mouth, I felt her hand along my huge erection, which now begged to be released from my shorts. I pulled away from our kissing and gazed down at her face, where I discovered a flicker in her eyes that held uncertainty. "You okay, Butterfly?"

"I'm a virgin." She sucked in a deep breath before continuing her thought. "You feel…huge, and now…I'm nervous." Her loud declaration dropped off to merely a soft whisper after an exasperated breath. So I guess it was anxiety I saw in her expression.

I didn't know whether to take her comment about my size as a compliment or feel like a world-class jerk because I had completely overlooked that thought that she might be a virgin. *Of course she's a virgin, you idiot! She's never had a boyfriend before.*

I could feel my dick soften from the realization that I was

an asshole. "We don't have to have sex. That is a first I want you to be completely ready for."

She smiled at my response and resumed rubbing my erection through my shorts, making my dick salute back to full attention. "There is another first I would like to try though, if you show me how." She slipped her small yet warm hand inside my shorts and stroked the length of my shaft.

"You want me to show you how to give a hand job?" My voice squeaked like a pre-pubescent teenage boy.

She pulled on the elastic waistband of my shorts and shoved them down along with my boxers to reveal my engorged hard-on springing free. "No. I want my mouth on you." She grabbed hold of the firm shaft with her hand and licked the pre-cum on the tip.

I swear I thought I would ejaculate at any second and shoot a load all over myself from just that one touch. "Lex, you don't have to do that..." But before I determined how to finish my thought, her mouth was sucking me.

"My God, Lex. I don't have to show you anything. You're doing a great job without any guidance." I moved her hand to the base of my shaft and encouraged her to slide her hand up and down while I remained in her mouth. I didn't last long. It only took a minute before my hot seed filled her mouth. She didn't gag or hold back. She held on while I pumped myself harder into her mouth, riding out the havoc-wreaking orgasm. It was a long time coming...literally. I couldn't remember the last time I had spewed myself with such a force.

She withdrew her mouth and hand. When she swallowed, I thought I'd come all over again because holy hell, that was hot. If I felt this amazing with just her mouth, how would feel when I was balls deep inside her? Then I reminded myself that she was a virgin. Crap. She was a virgin.

After a quick trip to the bathroom for each of us, presumably for a hurried clean-up, we returned to the kitchen area for our pizza dinner. She grabbed my discarded T-shirt from the floor and her underwear to slip into while I slid back in my shorts without the added confines of my boxers.

We sat and ate pizza in comfortable silence. The kind of silence you have with your best friend. Neither of us had to say anything. We were both obviously starving the way we devoured slice after slice. With our bellies contently full, we retreated to the living room sofa to watch some TV. It really didn't matter what we were watching. It was just so good to have her curled up next to me. My dream would be to have my life just like that every day.

I didn't realize how much I missed having Lex sleep next to me until the next morning when I had to leave for work. It was the first time in my life that I didn't want to get out of bed and get my day started. I wanted to stay in the warmth of my covers with my girlfriend's body snuggled up against me.

But even though it was a struggle, I still managed to pry myself away from the sleeping beauty and get myself to work. I left her a note, and right before lunch, I received a text that she had gone to her apartment to shower and change. Envisioning her naked in the shower would have me sporting another hard-on before long, so I tried to push down that thought.

I decided I needed a distraction, so I drove to Charlie's apartment during my lunch break. Even though I had my own key, I still knocked before entering, unaware of when or how I might find Louis, who seemed to have taken up residence with her between his shifts at work as a fireman.

"Get in here and tell me what happened." Charlie wasted

no time asking how I was doing, or why I was there to see her.

Louis was on the couch eating a sandwich when I entered her apartment. I took a seat on the loveseat so Charlie could sit next to her boyfriend. "I need some advice." I was silent for a beat, knowing they would patiently wait for me to purge my thoughts. Willing myself to remain soft-spoken and not freak out, I inhaled a deep, cleansing breath before confessing something so incredibly personal to my two confidants. "I want to have sex with Lex so badly, but she's a virgin. And I don't think that I have *ever* had sex with someone who hasn't done it before." It was true. The girls I messed around with in high school and college were definitely experienced. I was even sure that my first ever girlfriend, Cassidy, had sex with other guys before the first time we had sex. Even when *I* was a virgin, I didn't have sex with a virgin. Between blurting out my admission and the hurried thoughts dancing around my head, I was on the verge of panicked hysteria.

I tried to decipher what my best friends were thinking. I thought for sure they would laugh at me, given my heightened mania, but instead, Louis drew his brows together, and Charlie pursed her lips. I wasn't sure which was worse: having them poke fun at me or being the victim of their concerned looks.

"Are you two going to say something? I need help here."

"First of all, you need to just relax." Usually, Charlie was the one who would stress out, and I'd have to talk her off the ledge. She wasn't the greatest at calming me down, but right now, she was my best shot.

"Relax? Lean Bean, that's your advice?" I scrubbed the sides of my face with my hands. Her de-escalation methods were not working.

"Brother, she's right. If you're uptight and stressed, it

won't be good for you or Alexis." I heard Louis's words between his chewing, but that realization made me feel even more stressed.

"Maybe you just need some alcohol. Then you'd both be relaxed." Charlie had a point.

"Are you crazy? Too much alcohol, and he won't be able to get it up." Louis had a point, too.

"Is that even true? I don't know that there is ever truly that much alcohol for a man wanting to get laid to *not* be able to get the job done." *Why did I think it was a good idea to talk to them about this?*

"Maybe a drink or two would work, though," Louis said, still eating that damn sandwich. I realized my own stomach rumbled with hunger pains. I drove directly to their apartment, rather than stopping at a drive-thru along the way to pick up lunch.

I raised up from the cushions of the love seat and walked toward Charlie's kitchen. I figured I might as well make lunch for myself while I was there. "So I guess I should buy a bottle of wine?" I asked while pulling out the lunch meat from the fridge.

Charlie followed me to her kitchen and leaned against the counter. "That might work. I think she likes white wine. At least that's what she drank and Mom and Dad's."

I'd noticed that at Sunday dinner also.

"So should I do a dry one like a chardonnay, or a sweet one like a Moscato?"

I might've asked my sister's opinion, but Louis chimed in. "What the hell happened to you?"

Within in a split second, Louis, who unfortunately still had me by a few inches, was suddenly looming next to me.

"What has this girl done to your confidence? Where's the confident guy who kicked me out of his place so he could have the apartment to himself for a night of whatever you were planning to do with that chick?" He shoved my shoulder. I watched him push me and didn't even try to dodge it. "I think you need an intervention. You need to remember you are Cam Callahan."

"Louis, leave him alone." Charlie forcefully pulled her boyfriend back away from me with a fury, but then she gazed in my direction with a star-struck, sappy, gooey look in her gray eyes. "I think it's sweet that he's in love."

"You are jumping to extremes. I wouldn't go that far." *I mean, I want to spend the rest of my days with Lex, but did that actually translate to love?*

"Holy crap! You are in love." Excitement filled Louis's booming voice, and then he happily pushed me again, as evidenced by the shit-eating grin he wore. "Time for you to join the club of suckers."

"Hey!" Rather than pushing or pulling, as the two of them had taken to during this conversation, Charlie resorted to playfully slapping Louis's arm like she used to do when we were kids. I guess old habits die hard. They both exchanged adoring looks, and I thought I would puke on the sandwich I had just finished making.

"Can you guys tone down the PDA a bit for me?" I cringed before lifting the bread to my mouth and taking a bite of my lunch.

Their eyes bounced back and forth between each other before laughter erupted.

"What the hell is so funny?" My mouth was full of meat, bread, and cheese, so my voice was muffled and garbled as I spoke, trying not to spit out food at the crazy pair during their fit of giggles.

"You came over here to talk about sex, but a little flirtatious banter is too much for you?" She let another small chuckle escape before continuing her thought. "Be nice, or I won't tell you what Alexis said to me about this subject."

I dropped my food on a paper towel. "She said something to you?" I swallowed the last bite I had taken and tried not to choke. I needed a drink to help it slide down my throat, but I didn't want to pause and pull a bottle of water from her fridge. "What the hell did she say?"

"I'm not sure if I should say. She's my best girlfriend now." She stood, looking awfully confident for the interrogation I was about to give her.

I exchanged a glance with Louis, and he nodded. He knew exactly what I was thinking without needing to say anything. Granted, Charlie and I had a twin connection, but Louis and I had our own telepathy. He grabbed Charlie's arm, and I grabbed the other. Together, we lifted her up with her feet dangling and carried her over to the couch as she squealed. Then, we sat her down and began to poke at her sides until her giggles turned into full fits of laughter.

"Okay, I'll tell you." She yelped and squealed as she tried to catch her breath. I looked at Louis, and we both relented. "She's planning to give you her V-card this weekend."

"Lean Bean! Why didn't you tell me sooner? I thought you didn't keep secrets from me." My voice raised several octaves, making me squeak like a desperate fool.

"Are we the kind of siblings who talk about sex?" Her erratic breathing settled, and her gray eyes questioned me with the slight squint she shot my way.

"I believe you started it." I lifted my brow and turned my head toward the direction of her boyfriend.

"You talked to your brother about having sex with me?" Louis sucked in a surprised gasp at her, and she merely shrugged. "What the hell did you tell him, Charlene?" Louis very rarely called Charlie by her given name, but when he did, it was blatantly obvious the severity of the situation. His tone accelerated from shock to frustration quickly. He was irritated.

I figured I could offer some assistance by providing a simplified explanation, so I clapped Louis on his back. "She told me you were a jackass, but she didn't want me to kill you." I glanced at Charlie and then darted my eyes back at Louis. They truly were the best friends a guy could ever ask for. "It was difficult for me to hear about you two like that, honestly, but if I had to hear about the two of you and your sexual encounters so that you both could end up together, I would sit through the torture again."

The three of us let our gazes bounce back and forth with each other before laughter ensued again, covering me in the warmth of our friendship. My brain and heart were flooded with happy childhood memories of laughter with these two.

"Alexis is my friend now, but you are my favorite person —sorry, Louis. I won't keep secrets from you again. I promise." My sister hugged me like I needed to be comforted. I wish Lex was as open about revealing secrets as my sister is.

Lex wanted to stay at her apartment after karaoke, so I packed my bag and headed over to her place to pick her up on the way to the bar. One of these days, we could hopefully live together so we wouldn't be packing every time we spent the night with each other. The living together situation was going well for Charlie and Louis, so I didn't see why it wouldn't work for Lex and me. Maybe I'd talk to her about that soon. Maybe we could even get a bigger place that had two bedrooms.

When we arrived at the bar, it was still early, so we could secure a booth for the four of us. Lex and I snagged the table while waiting for Charlie and Louis to arrive a few minutes after us.

Our waitress came over with a binder full of songs and

took our drink order. Lex ordered a Jack and diet cola, while the rest of us ordered beer. I made a mental note about her choice of alcohol.

The bar became more and more crowded as patrons trickled in. We ordered burgers and drank our beverages and were having a great time together. The karaoke portion of the evening was about to start, so the girls decided to take a trip to the bathroom before our names were called.

The girls slid out of the booth and were about to make their way to the ladies' room when I spotted Lex holding her drink. "You can't be separated from your drink even to pee, Butterfly?" I pointed to the glass in her hand.

"I always take my drink with me." She looked at me, and a reverent silence followed.

Fortunately, my sister interjected. "Cam is a great drink watcher, Alexis. I promise, it's safe with him."

So now I understood. All those times in college when Charlie had me hold her drink for her when she went to the bathroom was so a guy wouldn't slip anything in it. I would have killed the guy who would even try, but that was beside the point. Alexis only depended on herself; she never trusted anyone to look out for her.

"You don't have to carry your drink with you when you are with me." I reached toward her and grasped the glass from her hand. "I promise that I will always look out for you."

She loosened her grip around the tumbler, and I returned her beverage to the tabletop. My two favorite women scurried off to the ladies' room, and Louis and I were left to ourselves.

"I never thought I'd see the day when Cam Callahan was head over heels in love." *What the hell kind of comment is that?*

"We haven't been dating that long. I wouldn't say I'm in love with her." I was pretty sure I was lying. I wasn't sure if I was being dishonest to Louis, or just denying the truth to myself.

"Being in love isn't a bad thing." He took a swallow of his beer. "I found that denying it doesn't work. It catches up to you…and when it does, it's actually pretty amazing."

"When did you get all mushy? You sound like a freaking girl." I shot a hard look his way. "But I'd say you and Lean Bean look pretty happy, so I guess it's worked out okay for you two. I don't want to tell her and scare her off. Look what happened the first time you told my sister."

"You're right. Maybe I should've asked Charlie out on a date before confessing my feelings to her. I got the order wrong. But you are Alexis's boyfriend. You can tell her." He took another swallow from his beer while the first karaoke singer took the stage.

Charlie and Lex returned in time to hear an amazing rendition of a Whitney Houston song by a thin, curly-haired woman who looked like she was in her mid-thirties. Unfortunately, my name was called next. I wasn't sure how I was expected to follow the voice that the crowded restaurant just heard, but after gulping down the rest of my beer in two swallows, I took my place on stage.

My parents loved their eighties and nineties music, so my sisters and I had to listen to a lot of those songs growing up. I chose an REO Speedwagon song that I knew all the lyrics to. I locked eyes with Lex the entire time I sang, and when I belted out *Can't Fight This Feeling*, I felt like I was singing straight from my heart and soul.

When I returned to the table, a vaguely sensuous light passed between us. There was an undeniable dark desire within Lex's eyes as she dragged her gaze seductively up and down my body. So when she whispered that she was ready to leave, I practically threw some cash at my sister and Louis before quickly racing out the door. Lex was right on my heels.

Even with the thought of getting back to her place as fast as possible, we recognized that the safest bet was to call an Uber. We decided she could just drive me back to my truck tomorrow. The minutes ticked by slowly until the arrival of the car and driver. But soon, we were on our way to her apartment.

The prolonged anticipation was almost unbearable. Just getting inside her place without ripping each other's clothes off was an accomplishment, because if I thought I'd been insane with wanting her previously, it was no match to what I was feeling at that moment. Our mouths were on each other before we managed to get the door open. Lex fumbled with her keys for several attempts until I took over and accomplished the task.

The door seemed heavier than expected when I shoved it out of our way, but again, it may have been due to the intense need I had to relieve the pressure that had been building in my jeans since we left the bar. She tugged at my shirt, and I broke away from our dancing tongues long enough to yank the cotton material over my head.

She took to trailing light kisses along my chest. Her lips were warm, and when her tongue flicked over one of my nipples, I scooped her into my arms and headed toward her bedroom. I tried to gently ease her onto the bed, but my self-control was extremely limited. I dropped her onto the mattress, and she bounced slightly on that comforter of butterflies. She pulled me down over her, and I nibbled at her soft earlobe while pushing the tank top she had worn to the bar over her head and tossed it somewhere.

Her pink, lacy bra was revealed, and as pretty as it was, I couldn't wait to get it off her. She arched her back, and I reached around for the clasp. She let a soft moan escape when I released her breasts from the confines of her undergarment. Shoving the lacy material off her, I initiated my attempt to thoroughly caress and worship her soft mounds. I cupped them with my hands and brushed my fingertips across her nipples. When she began to whimper, I moved my mouth from her ear and jawline to the swollen peak of her breast. I suckled and she wriggled beneath me.

"I need you now." Her smoky blue eyes smoldered, and her arousal was apparent. "I want you inside me. Please," she hissed with desperation and shimmied her shorts and panties off without any assistance from me. Still paying attention to her nipples with my tongue, I slipped my finger between her slick folds and entered her. When I rubbed her sensitive nub with my thumb, she flinched, and a slow moan vibrated from within her. After I inserted another finger, warm fluid slicked my movements.

Her channel pulsated, and I could feel she was getting close to the edge. With her orgasm being on the brink, my own arousal intensified to the point that I didn't think I could withstand any more patience. I heard her utter the word *now,* prompting me to withdraw my fingers from inside her and reach into the front pocket of my jeans for a condom.

No wonder my erection was so incredibly painful. My damn jeans were holding my expanding arousal captive. Wanting to spring it free, I fumbled for the button to release and pulled at my zipper with a loud grating sound. The teeth of the zipper finally parted and offered me some relief from the building pressure.

Before I could remove my pants and don the condom, my eyes connected with hers. Something in her expression had changed. She no longer appeared full of desire. Apprehension clouded her eyes, and her facial features hardened. "Get off me." I heard the words, and I watched her mouth move, but I didn't realize what she was saying. She appeared terrified or angry. I couldn't identify which emotion was there. Stark fear glittered in her eyes, but bridled anger infused her voice.

"I said get off me!" Her wailing scream rang throughout the room as she flattened her palms on my chest and tried to shove me away from her.

She wasn't successful in pushing my weight, but I willingly eased myself away from her to give her some space. My heart sank as she pulled at her bedspread and clutched it across her chest to cover her naked body. I stared at her in disbelief. I wasn't sure what happened. "Butterfly…" I tried to brush my hand across her face, but she flung my arm away.

"Get out of my apartment."

I stood up from her bed as she laced her last comment with venom. "Lex, what's going on?" I was certainly disappointed that I wasn't going to feel what it was like to be inside her, but I was hurt that something had happened and she wouldn't talk to me.

"I told you I wasn't going to have sex with you." Her demeanor had shifted so drastically that she was now a completely different person than the one I had just been making out with a few moments earlier.

"Lex, we don't have to make love tonight." Determination fed my need to sit back down next to her as she gripped her bedspread tighter. "Because whenever that time is, it won't be just sex. I love you. I love you like I never thought I could love another person."

Her eyes shimmered with water only a moment before a river of tears flowed over their brims and slid down her cheeks. "Well, I don't love you." Sadness painted her features, but I still couldn't believe how cold and distant she sounded. "Being around you, Cam, doesn't make me happy. It reminds me of my crappy childhood. My childhood doesn't bring back good memories for me. I have seen terrible things. I have done despicable things. It was a horrible time in my life, and unfortunately, you were a part of that time in my life. I have tried my best to move past that. I went to college, I have a career that I love, and for the first time in my life, I actually have friends."

Her emotional wounds tugged at my heart. "I'm your friend too, Lex."

"But yet, nearly every time I'm around you, I find myself in tears. Do you have any idea how long it's been since I cried this much?" She shook her head, willing embarrassment and shame to vanish. "I was a kid. I don't cry like that anymore."

I attempted to reach for her again, but she rolled away, out of my grasp.

"I said I wanted you to leave. Now get out of my apartment." She abruptly stood, still wrapped in that damn comforter with her stormy blue eyes overflowing with a thunderstorm of sadness while anger infused redness into her cheeks.

I heard what she was saying, but more than anything, I wanted her to understand that my new job in life was to make her happy. If she wasn't going to be happy around me, then maybe I needed to give her some space. Now that I had her back in my life, I wasn't going anywhere. I would back off for a bit, but it certainly wasn't going to be forever.

I left her place, but not before I heard her sobbing loudly as I exited. The whole situation definitely sobered me up, but I didn't have my truck to drive home. So I had to call Louis. Since he was with Charlie, I'd have to explain all of this to her also.

I tried all weekend to call Lex. She didn't pick up. I left two voicemail messages begging her to call me. I sent a few text messages also. Okay, so maybe a dozen or so texts. So much for giving her space.

By the time Monday arrived, I felt physically ill. My muscles ached, my throat was sore, and I had a throbbing headache. I called out of work so I could wallow and sleep all day. On Tuesday morning, the hangover effect still riddled my body even though I hadn't had a drop of alcohol since Friday night. The intense misery yielded another sick leave day for me, because I decided I wasn't going to work again. With that realization confirmed, I poured myself a beer for breakfast. I always heard that was the best cure for a hangover, and that was certainly how I felt.

I had never missed a day of work, so I wasn't entirely surprised when my sister and Louis showed up at my apartment. Well, that, and I hadn't responded to any of my sister's calls or texts either. I knew she would worry, but I couldn't seem to get out of the hole of self-pity I had taken refuge in to think about anyone else other than Lex.

"Really, Cam? Drinking at ten in the morning? What the hell?" Charlie abruptly snatched the bottle from my hand as she busted into my living room and found me in a heap on my couch.

She poured the beer down the kitchen sink while Louis grabbed a bottle of water from my fridge.

"I'm not drunk, Louis. That was the first I've had since Friday."

He unscrewed the cap from the water bottle and took a swallow. "I wasn't getting water for you. I'm thirsty, and you still don't keep any damn soda in your fridge."

With as lousy as I felt, I managed to let go of a quick burst of laughter. I was exhausted, so the smile that I had let slip had quickly faded, and I closed my eyes and relaxed into my couch. I wasn't in that position long before Charlie was slapping my cheeks and shoving my shoulders. I opened my eyes and gently pushed her arm away. I didn't want to hurt her, but she was annoying me.

"You need to pull yourself together." She plopped onto the couch on one side of me, while Louis took a seat on my other side, effectively wedging me between the two of them.

"What the hell is this? An intervention?" I turned my head to one side toward my sister and then swiveled in the other direction at my best friend.

"Hell yes, it is," she said bluntly but held an expression of concern on her face.

"You look like hell, Callahan." Louis didn't hold the same compassion. He was very matter of fact.

"I'll be back in thirty minutes." Charlie jumped up quickly and exchanged a glimpse of determination with her boyfriend. "Louis is going to stay with you." She turned on her heel and was headed for the door when she peered back over her shoulder at me. "And for God's sake, Cameron, take a shower." Then she was gone.

11
ALEXIS

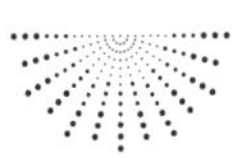

I cried all night on Friday. I understood that Cam didn't purposely try to hurt me, but I couldn't get past how I felt so vulnerable with him. I could also feel myself changing around him. That really seemed to knock me off-kilter. I wasn't sure how to make the situation I had created any better. I didn't work with Charlie again until Monday night, so I was actively trying to think about how I would explain things to her. She had texted me on Saturday, asking if I was okay. I was sure Cam had told her what had happened if she was inquiring about my well-being.

On Sunday, I received a text from Charlie, asking about Cam. I was driving, and while I shouldn't have looked down at my phone, I did. I'd seen too many accidents from texting while driving, but I still felt a compulsion to glance at my phone. I was aware of the consequences of that foolish act, so when I hit something in the road and felt my car swerve toward the shoulder, I figured I deserved whatever happened to me.

Luckily, I was able to slow down and make it safely off the road, out of the way of the traffic that whizzed by. I slammed the gearshift into park, annoyed with myself, and proceeded to get out of my car and survey the damage. I had a busted tire, which wasn't a big deal. Fortunately, I had learned how to change to a spare. I learned how to do a lot of things other women didn't, because I had always been used to relying solely on myself.

I cursed out loud. I had friends who truly acted like they cared about me, and I'd let the crap from my past ruin it for me. I tried hard not to think too much about my major screw-up while I hitched my car up on the jack. I had the last nut loosened from the wheel and was just about to pull the wheel with the flat off when a car pulled up behind mine.

"Great," I muttered to myself. I had unwisely left my bag with my knife in the car. What is more vulnerable than a woman stranded on the side of the road? *You know better than that, Alexis.* I blew out under my breath when I heard the footsteps approaching. I pulled the iron rod out of the jack and was ready to strike at the person moving toward me when I heard a familiar voice.

"You okay, Alexis?"

I quickly jumped to a standing position with the metal lug wrench still in my grasp.

I nodded and faced Cam's best friend. "Yep. Just a flat. Was changing it to the spare so I can haul the flat to get a plug popped in."

Something about his demeanor gave me the impression that he was slightly impressed. "If you want, we can throw the tire into my trunk, and I can drive you to get it repaired."

"No thanks. I'm good." I wiped my brow where my hair stuck to my forehead. It was late August, after all. "I've got it covered."

"I would really like to take you." He attempted to grab the tire iron from me, possibly due to the determined look I had on my face when he had originally approached me. "Charlie and Cam would never forgive me if I left you to fend for yourself on the side of the road."

He was probably right. I didn't want him to catch the wrath of his friends because of my stubborn nature. I swiped my hands on my shorts and reluctantly nodded in acceptance. Louis grabbed the wheel while I grabbed my purse and locked the doors.

I slid into the passenger seat of Louis' car and stared at my keychain. Being in the presence of his best friend and holding onto the Batman charm made me think of Cam, of course.

"He misses you, too." Louis was perceptive.

I remained quiet, not letting out my feelings. It was obvious he was speaking about Cam. I honestly did miss him. *What was wrong with me?* I had gone over the situation in my head over and over since asking him to leave. The truth of the matter was that I didn't have a clue what to say to him. He had called and sent text messages, but I had no idea how to respond. I wasn't sure what to say without giving away the dark secrets of my past. I swore to myself that I would *never* share those events with another soul.

"He's worried. The poor guy is in love with you."

I heard Louis talking, but I remained focused on the road passing by outside the window on my side of the car.

I guess Cam confessed his feelings about me to Louis. Again, I was sure this information would've been passed along to Charlie as well. The realization hit me that not only hadn't I figured out what I would say to Cam, but I hadn't decided what I would say to his sister, either.

Louis pulled into a service center and removed my flat from his trunk before I even moved from the passenger seat. I pushed open the door while Louis carried the tire toward the service desk. After explaining my situation, the attendant told us it would only be a few minutes, and he would have it as good as new.

Consequently, those were going to be the longest few minutes of my life. Silence doesn't necessarily make me uncomfortable, but watching how Louis judged me caused waves of restlessness to shake through every fiber of my being. Sure, I didn't usually care what people thought of me. But I had grown to care about Cam and Charlie and Louis. It reminded me of a situation my friend had helped me to understand a while ago.

When I was a brand-new nurse, there was an older nurse on day shift who'd given me a hard time. Her name was Carla. She had since retired from the emergency room, but I had to live with her opinions about me for several months. She would tell me that I basically sucked at my job, and that I would never be a good ER nurse.

One early morning when I was giving a report to Carla at the end of my shift, she told me it was evident that I wasn't progressing like I should be, and that she was going to tell the manager. I was crushed. Actually, I was devastated. Charlie had approached me in the parking lot as I walked to my car.

I didn't want to let on that Carla had upset me, but she was perceptive. She had heard the verbal assault on my credibility. So at that moment, when my confidence was shaken, Charlie had said to me, "Carla isn't a great ER nurse. She shouldn't condemn anyone." I turned to her showing that I appreciated her effort, but I was sure that my body language showed my defeat. "If criticism comes from someone you respect, it's okay for you to do a little self-reflection. But if it comes from someone like Carla, you need to brush that stuff off. She sucks. Just let her go live her sucky life in misery, all alone."

I didn't respond to Charlie's wise words, but I had smiled at her. She returned the smile and waved goodbye.

So now, I had to relive my friend's words. I wouldn't care if anyone I didn't respect judged me. But knowing my friends were probably talking about me or disapproving of me hurt- - mostly because I deserved it.

"I'll always respect and admire you for saving my girlfriend's life." He stared straight ahead instead of looking in my direction as we stood in the garage, waiting for the service attendant to fix my tire. "I'm not sure what's going on exactly, but my best friend is hurting. I can also tell that you're hurting. Having survived some hurt in a relationship myself, please let me give you some advice." He turned to face me. "Letting go of your fear and letting someone love you is the key to happiness."

Thank goodness the attendant reappeared at that moment so I could break the eye contact Louis had established.

I managed to mutter a few *thank yous* to Louis before he watched me drive away with my freshly repaired tire back on my car. When Tiffany texted me, asking to switch shifts, I happily agreed. She wanted to work Monday and have off Sunday. I accepted the offer, knowing I would be able to prolong the time before being confronted by Charlie about her brother and me.

Since I didn't take a nap before my impromptu Sunday night shift, I crashed the moment I arrived at my apartment on Monday morning. Sleeping as hard as I did during daylight hours meant I was up most of the night on Monday without being able to get myself to fall back asleep. I last remembered looking at the time at around six o'clock, during the many hours of tossing and turning. My body didn't feel rested, so I presumed I hadn't been asleep very long when I heard loud pounding on Tuesday morning.

I thought it was my head pounding, but once I was jerked out of my slumber, I realized someone was knocking very loudly on my door. I glanced at the clock. Ten twenty-seven. I tossed the covers off and swung my legs over the side of my bed. The pounding continued as I trudged toward the front of my apartment when I began to hear a familiar voice.

"Alexis, open up. I need to talk to you." A sleepy fog still clouded my thoughts, so I wasn't thinking one hundred percent clearly. Certainly, if I had been able to conjure up a rational thought, I wouldn't have opened my door to a rather disgruntled Charlie.

Before it registered in my slumberless brain that she was furiously glaring daggers at me, she pushed into my apartment. I closed the door behind me and faced her. I braced myself, in preparation for receiving the brunt of her anger.

"He loves you. And you love him, so you are coming with me now."

"Uh, no," I scoffed.

"I swear to God, Alexis, you're coming with me, or I'm going to die trying to get you to." Her facial features were creased, and anger lit her gray eyes. "You'll have to stab me with that knife you like to carry in your purse, because you have avoided my brother long enough."

I weighed my options. I still hadn't a clue of what I would say to Cam, but it was also imminent that I would have to face him eventually. With the determined look on his sister's face, now was probably as good a time as any, I supposed.

"Okay." I had thought I would see a smug, satisfied smirk spread across her face. But instead, her features softened, and her lips tugged upward at the corners. Then she hugged me. She caught me off guard. I had witnessed her anger, fury, and frustration only moments earlier, but there she was, hugging the crap out of me. I nearly stumbled backward at her launching embrace.

"Please talk to him about whatever is going on. Just please *talk* to him."

I was pretty sure she was crying because she sniffled as she leaned into me. I could feel the utter sadness in her voice. I hadn't realized how many people would be affected by the ghosts haunting me.

As I rode in Charlie's car to Cam's apartment, I thought about Louis's words. *Letting go of your fear and letting someone love you is the key to happiness.*

Maybe I was truly just scared all along. Maybe I wasn't being brave by keeping everything in. Maybe I kept my memories bottled up out of fear. And maybe it was time to let someone love me. I glanced down the length of my body as Charlie inserted the key into the door of Cam's apartment. I hadn't bothered to change before leaving my place. I was wearing pajama pants and a spaghetti strap tank top with a soft, built-in bra. When the door swung open, I could hear my flip-flop-clad feet shuffle forward into his living space.

Intense astonishment crossed the chiseled features on his face. He stood before me, blank yet amazed and shaken. He was genuinely surprised to see me. I doubted he had planned for his sister to ambush me and drag me to see him. His dark hair was wet like he was fresh from the shower, and as he walked toward me, I could smell the woodsy soap he liked to use.

He halted his footsteps before getting within ten feet of where I stood. Those hazel eyes were infused with green flecks and swirled with emotion around an outline of light brown. Pain flickered in his slouched stance. As I sat in Charlie's car on the way over, I had imagined he'd be happy to see me. But here he was with an unreserved, melancholy appearance.

"I'm so sorry." His Adam's apple bobbed up and down as he swallowed. "Please forgive me." He clenched his fists at his side as he tried to withstand the urge to approach me further. "I love you so much, Butterfly. I can give you space. Just please don't shut me out altogether." The tenderness in his expression rippled a wave of guilt through me.

He really thought *he* had done something to me. I guessed it was time to set the record straight. Anxiety left a sour taste in the pit of my stomach as I realized it was time to let go of my fear. I tossed a sidelong glance at Charlie and Louis, who stood on opposite sides of the room. Charlie was still near the door, and Louis was next to the couch.

When I locked my gaze with Charlie's, she mouthed "thank you." When I turned my eyes to Louis, he approached me and said, "Don't be afraid…to call us if you need a ride home." He offered an extra nod and crossed the room to where his girlfriend was waiting. When they slipped out the door, I knew Louis had meant something different when he told me not to be afraid.

The door clicked shut behind me, and we were alone with a mere ten feet separating us. I wanted to let him hold me, because I could see he was truly fighting his self-restraint. But I needed to tell him. He needed to hear all about me before I could truly let him love me.

So I took in a deep, cleansing breath and blew it out as Cam watched me mentally prepare myself for the revealing of my sorted past. "I'm finally ready."

Cam's eyes questioned my statement, but he made no attempt to speak. His stare weighed heavily with concern, and those amber orbs continued to wordlessly dig into me.

"You should probably sit down."

Without any hesitation, he quickly responded to my request by taking a seat on the couch.

The silence from him during the already tense moment crippled me. I needed to find a way to tell him about my appalling previous life. Worry was sketched across his face, so I needed to pull courage from somewhere. I wanted to let go of the heaviness in my chest and the burdens of my past. Pent-up emotions of pain and anger simmered within me, and they were about to come to a full boil. The buildup from sharing the angst I suffered was about to erupt, and I needed one final moment to console myself before I blurted out the misery of the night that still haunted me.

"His name was Dragon."

Lines of confusion deepened along his brow and under his eyes. I could tell he was internally debating whether to ask a question or allow me to continue without interruption, so I moved forward with my explanation.

"He tried to rape me when I was seventeen."

"Butterfly..." Choked emotion laced his voice, and I swear I saw water collecting in those memorizing, gorgeous, hazel eyes. I wasn't sure why I started with the Dragon incident. There had been so much in my past that it probably would've made more sense to begin in some sense of chronological order.

"He attacked me. Even though I fought him off, I distinctly remember the sound of him releasing his zipper. I have that sound somehow tattooed in my brain, and when I heard it the other night..."

"I'm so sorry, Butterfly." His soft, amber gaze followed me as I paced back and forth in his living room. His twitching muscles were an obvious giveaway that he wanted to stand up, but he stayed in place per my request.

Cam told me that it was okay to need people sometimes. I knew in my heart that he was right. Because spilling confessions and tales from my prior life definitely had me needing him. I was trying to be brave and share painful memories of my past, but I needed to be near him. I felt compelled to have his heated embrace wrap around me and comfort me. I actually needed a hug for what seemed like the first time in my life.

So I plopped myself next to him and sank into the cushion. Our thighs brushed against each other. Cam continued to look straight ahead, but once I leaned into him, he wrapped his strong arms around me. The warmth from his presence covered me like a cozy blanket with a promise to keep me safe and protected. My head rested against his chest, and a brief kiss grazed the top of my head. He gently rubbed my scalp with his hand, and my ramrod posture began to relax.

"I didn't mean what I said the other night…about not being happy around you." I swallowed hard, still leaning against the fresh smell of his cotton t-shirt. "It is true that I haven't been happy for most of my life. But being around you has made me happier than I ever thought possible."

"Your happiness is very important to me, Lex. I love you." A gentle squeeze caressed my shoulders following his words. I actually believed him. Honesty was infused in his caring voice.

"So as I explained to you before, my dad was abusive to my mom. Fortunately, he left when I was ten." I continued to take refuge in the warmth surrounding me. "But she found a new abusive boyfriend before too long."

He remained mute, but he continued to rub my head and comfort me without words. His presence was soothing enough. I didn't need him to speak. Just being with him was all I needed.

"When I was sixteen, I just couldn't stand by and watch anymore. So I pulled a kitchen knife on the jackass when he had my mom cornered and was beating the crap out of her."

His body stiffened slightly next to me, but he still didn't utter a sound.

"I stabbed him several times, and then I left…I ran away."

The sound of his gulping air echoed in my ears before he squeezed me tighter. I could tell he wanted me to continue my story, so I refocused and progressed forward.

"I was homeless after that. I lived out of my car for nearly two years." I pulled out of his embrace and found his hazel eyes as if he could possibly provide me with some kind of redemption. "I was never charged with assault. I honestly don't know what happened to either of them."

"Geez, Lex. I had no idea you had lived such a tumultuous life." His eyes pleaded with me to finish my tale of misery, even though this information noticeably left him pain-stricken.

"During that time, I was attacked by Dragon. That wasn't his real name," I explained. "When you're homeless, you don't actually give anyone your given name. Either you make one up, or others select one for you. When he assaulted me, I stabbed him multiple times."

"My God, Butterfly." He pulled me into him again, smashing my face against his shoulder.

"When you're homeless, no one *sees* anything. No one reported Dragon's stabbing, but that incident earned me my nickname. Quicksilver." Having said the words out loud made me realize just how much my life sounded like a horrible embarrassment. "But as soon as I could, I moved into a cheap apartment and went to college."

Freeing myself from those haunting ghosts had me feeling a thousand times lighter. Letting go of all the shadows of my past really felt quite liberating...that whole *getting the weight off my shoulders* analogy actually rang true. I just wasn't sure at what cost I just disclosed my secrets.

"I hope you'll forgive me." I lightly brushed my fingertips along his forearm. "I hope I haven't destroyed us." Somehow, I found the strength after spewing out things I kept hidden for an entire lifetime to look back at the man who completely changed my mind about how I envisioned the world.

However, seeing the despair in his features had me believing that we wouldn't recover from what I just confessed. Sorrow and disappointment creased his brow. He exhaled, and I prepared myself for the rising dismay covering us.

"Lex, I'm not going to lie, I've been destroyed these last few days. You were on my mind so much that I couldn't go to work. I couldn't go to the gym. I'm not even sure if I ate, slept, or showered." He swept the stray hair away from my face, and my heart rate increased. "But if I'm being honest, I've been happily destroyed by you for a while now." That damn hazel gaze fired with intensity, and I froze, awaiting his next words. "I'm emotionally invested in us. I haven't been able to stop thinking about you since I saw that butterfly tattoo on your hip. I haven't gone anywhere or done anything without thoughts of you dancing around in my head."

The brick of guilt and disappointment in the pit of my stomach eased. Regret could no longer hold me back from letting people into my life. "Cam, it actually feels so good to get everything off my chest. I've been broken for so long, but I want to move forward. I'm just not sure how long it will take for me to feel like a whole person again." I honestly hadn't felt like I'd been living a whole life until recently.

"You're not broken, just emotionally bruised. Broken implies that you need to be fixed, but you just need time to heal." Cam rubbed my shoulders, and my relaxed state began to return to me. "I promise I won't ever try to fix you. And I'll patiently wait while you take the time you need to heal. Just please, please let me be here…in your life and, maybe, someday in your heart." He pointed to the left side of my chest and briefly brushed his lips against mine.

It was a memory that would last with me for a very long time. "And you're already in my heart. Batman took up residence there a long time ago." I gently kissed his lips again. "And Cam has been in here," I said, pointing to the same spot on my chest. "For a lot longer than when Batman found Butterfly girl again. You were in my heart the first moment you offered me coffee at work…and I don't even like coffee." Tears blinded my eyes and choked my voice. But I it would be okay, because the tears were happy ones. "I have one more confession to make."

"You can tell me anything, Lex." His facial features softened, and his jaw relaxed.

"I lied about something else on Friday night." Hot tears slid down my face, tickling my cheeks. "I told you I don't love you. But I do. I love you like I never knew existed." I swallowed hard to smother the sob that surfaced. "I love you like I can't live without you, or I-might-die kind of love." I swear I saw his amber eyes glisten with tears. "I love you like I want to be with you all the time and never spend a moment apart."

Then, no longer holding back, he crashed his lips against mine with the promise of a future devoid of secrets.

12

CAMERON

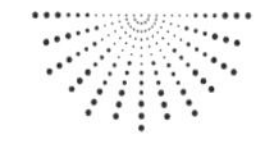

It's been one week since Lex and I agreed to never keep secrets from each other. And it's been one week since we agreed to spend the night together every night she wasn't at work. Louis and I visited the girls one night last week, and we planned to visit them again tonight.

On weeknights, Lex stayed at my place so I could get up and get ready for work in the morning. But over the weekend, we stayed at hers. I did love her butterfly comforter. I had already been thinking about moving in together, even though we hadn't let our make-out sessions progress beyond kissing this last week.

I hated that I had to spend *any* night away from her, but at least I could sneak into the ER to see her one night a week and bring her hot chocolate. Louis picked me up from my apartment around ten, and we headed to the drive-thru for coffee and cocoa.

I was always happy going to see Charlie. I certainly used to enjoy the attention her female colleagues would give me. Now, I only wanted Lex to flirt with me and give me sexy smiles. My pulse still quickened when I knew I'd see her soon. The anticipation of being with her caused that warm, intoxicating feeling to course through my veins.

I also didn't mind the Charlie and Louis situation as much now that Lex and I were together. We actually made a pretty good foursome. I wished that we could've been a foursome a long time ago, but I was smart enough to realize that things between Lex and I had to wait and develop into what it was now after the long journey we'd been forced to take without each other.

I was really glad that Lex and Charlie had one another as well. My sister never had a female confidant before, and my girlfriend hadn't had too many friends at all, so the two of them had a special bond. They talked on the phone and hung out together, and it was good to see their relationship develop into an amazing friendship. I would be lying if I didn't say that I missed all the time that Charlie and I used to spend together, but now that we had other special people in our lives, I think we were happier overall.

When Louis reappeared, I thought that was the best thing that had happened to Charlie and me. But now that Lex reentered my life, I was certain that was the most significant, defining moment of my life. I was positive I would spend the rest of my days with her. It might sound cliché, but we had a one-in-a-million connection. We were soul mates. Obviously, choosing to sit next to her on the school bus was a turning point also. I was destined to have her with me...just like Louis chose Charlie and me. I still think he chose me first, but I'm not sure if that's how they remembered it.

As Louis and I walked through the sliding glass door into the ER, it was eerily quiet. I wouldn't dare say the Q word out loud. According to Louis, Charlie, and Alexis—all who were emergency medical personnel—saying the Q word would bring about some kind of disastrous tornado of events. Then the devil himself would drop out of the sky and a fireball of havoc would wreak onto the emergency room. So I wouldn't say the word. But it felt creepy. It was too quiet.

Tiffany waved to Louis and me once we approached the triage window. The wooden door to the ER swung open so that my friend and I could enter the main part of the department. I distributed coffee cups to Tiffany, Carolyn—who was the charge nurse tonight—and of course, my sister. Charlie happily grabbed the cup out of the cardboard carrier, and without even saying thank you, she was giving goo-goo eyes to Louis.

I searched for the woman who was firmly rooted in my heart as I continued to hold her large hot chocolate in the last occupied cup holder of the cardboard carrier. But before I was able to lay eyes on my butterfly girl, I heard her. However, the voice of the woman I loved screeched through the air after a thunderous crash and a loud slap resonated against the tiled floor. "I need some help over here!"

Hearing my girlfriend yell that she needed help sent me running in the direction of that voice faster than rest of the ER personnel. I didn't recognize the area of the department where she was. But as I ran to Lex, I saw a man in a white coat collapsed on the floor next to her.

"I feel like we've done this before," Louis said to Charlie very nonchalantly. I remembered hearing the story of the old man who had collapsed in front of them in the grocery store. They seemed pretty calm for recognizing that bad luck presented itself in front of them at least twice now.

"We make a good team, Coleman." She gave Louis one quick wink while Tiffany and Carolyn rolled a stretcher close to the fallen man.

"*Ohmigod,* Dr. Collins!" Tiffany shrieked as she recognized the man on the ground as the physician on duty in the ER that night.

"Cam, help me lift him onto the stretcher," Louis said, and I complied. I grabbed his legs while he scooped his arms through the doctor's armpits, and we hoisted him onto the gurney.

The six of us quickly rolled the stretcher into an exam room and began to perform CPR and advanced life support measures. As an athletic trainer, I was trained in CPR, but the more advanced skills involved in saving someone's life were foreign to me. I could ice down injuries and wrap an ankle, and even diagnose a concussion, but a collapsed player without a pulse needed a paramedic as fast as humanly possible.

So without a doctor able to act as the leader in this situation, that left Louis to assume the role. He was calm and organized a coordinated effort. He assigned each of us roles and communicated effectively. Dr. Collins wasn't breathing and didn't have a pulse, so my job was to provide chest compressions. Charlie attached a heart monitor to the physician's chest. Whatever heart rhythm was identified on the screen required a jolt of electricity to shock the heart back into a normal, effective rhythm. After a failed attempt, Tiffany inserted an IV catheter to administer him life-saving drugs. Lex was at the head of the bed, providing rescue breathing through a mask until Louis was able to slip a breathing tube into his windpipe and provide life-sustaining breaths and oxygen directly into his lungs.

Carolyn had called someone on her portable phone and was busy writing down the tasks we had completed. She offered to switch out compressions with me, but I felt bad having a woman do such physical labor. Fortunately, I was physically fit, but I still imagined I would be sore the next day. I was sure I wouldn't need to work out my arms for a few days.

Louis instructed me to hold off on compressions to get a

good reading on the cardiac monitor again. He called for everyone to remain clear of the patient while he delivered another jolt of electricity.

This time, the nurses and Louis seemed pleased by the resulting heart rhythm that danced across the monitor. Charlie pressed two fingers on the doctor's neck and reported, "He has a pulse."

After a simultaneous sigh of relief from the four nurses and Louis, I was instructed that I didn't need to resume compressions. Several minutes passed by, but everything seemed to move so quickly that things proceeded in a blur of rapid events. I heard talk about myocardial infarction, and cardiac cath lab, and calling staff in to open up a vessel in his heart.

Then, before I could even conceive how much time had elapsed, what time it was, or what was even happening, a team of people in scrubs wearing masks and surgical caps collected the stretcher and pushed Dr. Collins out of the ER. There were hugs exchanged and cheers exclaimed. Charlie and Louis kissed. Lex and I did as well. Carolyn informed us that another physician was on his way in to complete the shift. Apparently, the ER was on a divert pattern until the next doctor arrived, so no other patients could enter by ambulance or helicopter. There was some concern on what to do if a walk-in patient arrived, but the general consensus was to cross that bridge when it presented itself.

The oncoming physician thanked Louis profusely for his help. It was close to one in the morning, and I had to work at six forty-five, but I was too wound up to relax enough to go to sleep. So I invited Louis back to my apartment for a beer.

"You were amazing tonight. I don't know how you maintained your cool. I'm not sure how any of you did," I said to Louis as we sat in my apartment, each taking long swallows of beer.

"It's my job. I'm just glad we were there when he collapsed. He just as easily could've fallen while in the bathroom, and it could have been a really long before he was found."

"Well, out of all the crazy stuff I've seen you do, tonight definitely takes the cake. You saved that doctor's life." We'd received word that Dr. Collins survived the cardiac catheterization procedure and was able to have his occluded heart vessel re-opened.

Our phones simultaneously vibrated with an incoming text. It was the group chat with Charlie.

Charlie: The crisis response team came into the ER for a debriefing. Tiffany had a hard time getting herself together, so Carolyn sent her home after the debriefing.

Cam: You okay?

Charlie: Yes. Of course. My boyfriend is freaking awesome, so I'm basking in that right now. I've been listening to how he's a hero over and over again.

Louis: [smiley face with tongue sticking out]

Cam: Great. Now he's going to have to sleep on my couch. His head won't be able to fit out the door to leave.

Louis: I'll force it if I have to. I can't wait to see you at home in a few hours.

Cam: [puking emoji] Did you both forget I'm on this group chat?

Alexis: [GIF dancing] I love that I'm on the group text now too!

Charlie: [laughing emoji]

I hadn't realized Lex was on the group text. It was definitely a different dynamic now. It had been Charlie, Louis, and me for so long. Then it was just Charlie and me for the last five years. It was so good for our threesome to be back together, but with the addition of Lex, we had definitely transitioned from being three friends to two couples. I was okay with that. I felt like Lex was going to be part of our group from now on.

The following weekend was Labor Day weekend. The four of us decided to take a road trip to Williamsburg. It was only a three-hour drive, and we planned to visit the large amusement park there. Lex had never been to a carnival before I took her to one. There were lame-ass rides there, but she enjoyed herself, so I was excited to see what she thought of true roller coasters.

We arrived at the amusement park early on Friday evening. The crowd wasn't too bad, so we were able to ride a few roller coasters without having to wait terribly long. The air was humid, so the moisture hung low and thick. My clothes clung to my torso, and the hanging moisture had the hair surrounding Lex's face spiraling into little ringlets while the bulk of her hair remained pulled back into a ponytail. Her blue eyes remained wide with excitement the entire time we strolled through the park. I held her hand the traditional way as we walked, taking in the sights, sounds, and smells.

People-watching had been a long-time hobby of mine, so there were throngs of people for me to observe. I watched their body language and their mannerisms. I noticed Lex frequently fidget with the small purse she wore across her chest. I hoped she realized that I wouldn't ever let anything happen to her. Luckily, I told her that her bag would be searched before entering the park, so she would need to take out her pocketknife. I was certain that added to her inability to completely relax.

She was a people watcher, too. She was very attuned to how close someone was, and even if she wasn't looking, she was completely aware of someone's presence. With a crowd of people surrounding us at every turn, she was probably on a little bit of sensory overload. Her body language was somewhere between excitement and cautious. So I stopped walking and pulled her into a hug. Louis and Charlie continued their pace.

"I love you, Butterfly," I spoke directly into her ear as I leaned down with her against me. I wanted to make sure she heard me through the noise of the crowd.

She pulled her sparkling blue gaze up to me and displayed a broad smile. "I know." Then she placed her cheek on my chest and squeezed me tighter. "Thank you for everything."

I broke away from our embrace long enough to drag her away from the passing crowd to an area near the restrooms by a fountain statue. It was the kind of fountain that displayed a statue of a woman dressed in cloth spewing water out of her extended arms into a surrounding pool of water.

"If you haven't figured it out by now, I want to show you the world. I want to be there for all your firsts." I linked my thumb with hers in the way that was so special to us. "I can only pray that I make you as happy as you make me. You are my world." I looked into the depths of her eyes, and I could see the slightest quiver in her facial features. My God, I didn't want to make her cry. "I love our story. I love that I had the pleasure of being your first friend as a child, and I love that I get to be your first boyfriend. My parents adore you. Louis wants to look after you. And Charlie has her first female best friend. You make life perfect." Before I could finish my last thought, she was stretching up on the tips of her toes so she could and kiss me.

It definitely wasn't a chaste kiss. She kissed me like no one was watching. Maybe she was aware people were watching but didn't care. I certainly didn't care at that moment. I would gladly welcome her warm tongue into my mouth whenever the opportunity presented itself.

"Cam, I love that you have shared your life with me," she said when she finally broke away. She wasn't crying. She was smiling brightly at me. "My life sucked for a long time. You were the shining star in my darkness so many years ago. And now, you have let me spend some time in that wonderful life you have. You have shown me what friendship is by sharing your friends with me. You have shown me what it's like to have a family by sharing yours with me. And most of all, you have shown me love. I had no idea what love even was until you shared your heart with me. I'll never be able to tell you how very important you have become to me. But I will show you that I love you every chance I get. Because I do love you. I love you with every fiber of my being. I love you with the intensity of a rocket being launched into outer space. I'm eternally grateful that you have shared your life and your love with me."

I lifted our hands and kissed her fingers.

"I'm never going to walk away again. You're stuck with me now." Lex's lips pulled upward into the most adorable smile just as my phone vibrated in my front pocket. Lex pulled her cell out of her purse at the same time as I reached for mine. We received a text simultaneously.

Charlie: We are in line at the teacups. Hurry so we can ride together!

Cam: We'll be right there.

Louis: Where did you disappear to anyway?

Alexis: Went to see a fountain.

Louis: ???

Charlie: [puking face emoji]

I loved my circle of friends. Lex and I slipped our phones back into place, and I clutched her hand tightly as I led her to the teacups as quickly as I could maneuver through the walkways surrounded by people and vendors. We met up with Charlie and Louis in time to ride in the same cup together. Louis and I spun the teacup so fast that I thought Charlie might vomit. If Lex was nauseous, we never would've known. She was laughing too hard to let on.

Once the park closed for the night, darkness began to surround us. With only the light of the full moon and the surrounding stars, we strolled out of the park as two couples holding hands. After a late dinner, we went to our hotel rooms for some much-needed rest. Charlie and Louis had a room on the same floor as us but further down the hall. Lex and I walked into our room with our weekend luggage and took note of the two beds. She shot me a quizzical look.

"I hope you're planning to sleep under the covers with me."

I dropped my bag and moved to stand next to her in two strides. "This hotel was out of rooms with kings, so I had to settle for two queens. But make no mistake, I wouldn't care if this room came with twin beds. I would still be sleeping under the covers in the same bed as you."

She sighed with relief. I was so happy that she wanted to sleep alongside of me. Lex showered first, and then it was my turn. When I got out and slipped into clean shorts, I saw the woman I love collapsed on top of the quilt with her eyes closed. I reached for the blanket folded at the foot of the mattress and pulled it over her. Then I turned off the light and slipped beneath the same blanket. I would forever be a happy man if I could sleep next to Lex every night for the rest of my life.

The next morning, my girl was sleeping so soundly I hated to wake her. After several minutes of me watching her sleep, she must've felt my eyes on her because she awakened on her own.

After a quick kiss and a change out of our pajamas, we rode the elevator down, and met Charlie and Louis on the first floor of the hotel where they offered a breakfast buffet to guests. After gathering two plates of food, we joined Charlie and Louis at a table to eat breakfast. The two of them were nearing the end of their meal, but they stayed and talked with us a few minutes before getting up to leave.

"Hey, bro, give us fifteen minutes and we'll be ready to go. We need to go back upstairs for a little bit," Louis said, giving me a suggestive wink. *Gross.*

I swallowed a bite of my eggs and tried my best to keep the vomit creeping up my throat at bay. Louis grabbed my sister's hand and literally skipped away from our table. I was going to try really hard not to throw up.

"Where are they going?" Her question was innocent enough, but was she really that naïve?

"They're going to have sex." I hoped my bluntness would quickly cut off any further discussion on the matter.

"Does that bother you?" Again, her question was innocent, but really?

I gently placed my fork on the plate. "I'm super happy that my best friends are in a relationship. It has definitely been awkward at times, but I try to convince myself that seeing the two of them go off on their own isn't any different than it used to be when we were kids."

"How so?" She seemed genuinely interested, and she leaned in toward me as if she didn't want to miss a single word of my explanation.

"Those two had a great time keeping things from me. They would go fishing or exploring or swimming—just the two of them—when we were little. They thought I didn't know about it. At first, I was kind of bummed that they didn't include me in everything they did together, but I realized that there were times when Louis and I were alone together, or Lean Bean and I were alone together. Sometimes it was just better to pair up, rather than always have a threesome. But, then again, the saying *is*, 'two's company, three's a crowd.'"

"That was very mature of you," Lex said solemnly while taking a bite of cantaloupe. I enjoyed watching everything about her. The way she slept, the way she ate, the way she smiled at only me.

"That's how I actually ended up sitting on the bus next to you...the two of them wanted to sit together, so I became the odd man out. They've tried really hard to ensure that I don't feel like a third wheel anymore. But now that our threesome has become a foursome, it's better than I could've ever imagined." I reached across the table for her hand that still held her fork. She released the utensil with a loud clank as it fell to her plate, and she laced her fingers with mine.

"I think *we* need to go back up to our room for a little while." Her blue eyes gave me an expression I'd seen once before...the night of our *almost* first time. I wasn't sure if I should react to the desire coming from across the table. I wanted to, but I didn't want to cause her pain, either.

"Are you sure?" I asked, uncertain what her response would be.

"I've never been so sure about anything in my life." She clasped a tighter grip on my hand. "I want you to show me how much you love me."

I tried to be cool, but my insides swirled relentlessly. I pulled her to a standing position, released her hand, and carried my plate to the dirty station. She was right next to me. Even when I didn't see her, I sensed her presence just like I have always been able to do.

We walked toward the elevator and rode quietly to our floor. Still without saying words, I swiped the key card into the slot of our room and swung the door open. We stood facing each other once inside the room after the door clicked shut behind us for a brief moment in an attempt to throttle the intense desire crackling around us.

There was no need to fight the overwhelming need I had to touch her, so I took the single stride toward her and cupped her face.

"I want my first time to be with you."

I heard her whispered voice, but I couldn't find any words to respond. I needed to kiss her before I lost my ability to breathe. So I collided my lips with hers.

The kiss began slow and thoughtful, but as I moved my mouth over hers, devouring its softness, I probed my tongue at the seam. She gave in to the passion of our kiss freely and allowed me access to her warmth as her jaw opened. As I nibbled her bottom lip and explored the recesses of her mouth, her hands slipped under my shirt, and I felt her fingertips glide up my abdomen and to my chest.

I released the hold I had on her face and moved them to the small of her back. "Can…you…take…your…shirt…off?" she huffed out during our fervid kissing.

I broke the sucking seal of our lip-lock to answer. "I will, if you will," I said with a jagged breath. Her swirling blue eyes held me captive as she pulled her shirt over her head. I grabbed ahold of mine, and it was on the floor as swiftly as I could manage.

She stood before me in a green, lacy bra. Green was my new favorite color. I was in mesh shorts, so when she slipped her hand into the waistband, she was able to access my growing erection quite easily. I really tried to maintain some composure, but I was out of my mind with the arousal she enveloped me in. She was the only woman I would ever want to be with again. She stirred feelings in me that I'd never experienced. I didn't just want her. I *needed* her.

As she held my shaft firmly in her hand while gliding it up and down, I resumed kissing her and reached behind her to unclasp her bra. A whispered moan escaped her lips, and I thought I might expel the load that had been building for weeks now.

With our mouths still connected and her hand still in my shorts, we shuffled closer to the bed. I grazed the tip of one of her nipples with my finger, and her next moan vibrated against her throat louder than the last. The backs of her legs hit the bed, and she tumbled backward, pulling her hand out of my shorts as she fell gently onto the mattress. So I didn't crush her, I laid next to her and closed my mouth against one of her nipples while stroking the other one with my thumb. She arched her back and wriggled against me.

Her desire was apparent, as was mine. She struggled to pull my shorts down, so I assisted by grabbing the loose elastic and yanking them off with one strong pull. My boxers left at the same time. My erection sprang forward as I began a trail of kisses from Lex's soft, round breasts down her belly. Her skin was so warm and soft, I just wanted to taste every part of her. I swirled my tongue around her belly button, and she nimbly pulled at the snap of her shorts. After the pop of its release, I pushed her shorts down her thighs. Once the legs of her shorts reached her knees, she kicked them onto the floor. Her green panties remained in place.

I pushed my finger into the last bit of clothing covering her. She gasped, and I slipped into her slick folds. Warmth and heated wetness surrounded my single digit. When I inserted another finger inside her channel, I could tell she was finally ready. I think she felt our time was that moment also. She looped her fingers into the waistband of her underwear and pulled them off. They flew across the room like a slingshot when she released them off the bottom of her feet.

I had to remove my fingers from inside her to retrieve a condom from my wallet. Lex watched me intently as I rolled it on. I couldn't remember ever feeling this rock hard in my life. I was incredibly engorged and had an unwavering feeling of spontaneous combustion brewing when I grabbed ahold of my erection and lined up with her entrance.

She was so incredibly tight. A whimper squeaked from her as I pushed myself deeper inside her snug passage. "Are you okay?" I asked while searching her eyes as I hovered over her.

"I'm more than okay. Show me how much you love me." Her near panting had me more turned on than ever.

After meeting slight resistance, I finished pushing my way into the sweet haven of her tight tunnel and paused for her to adjust to me. She wrapped her arms around me firmly, holding me in place as if I'd go anywhere…ever. As I thrust in and out of her now very slick channel, she met my rhythm and arched her back toward me, urging me deeper.

I felt myself getting closer and closer to the edge when her breathing quickened, and her inner core began to pulsate around my shaft. As she dug her fingernails into my back and huskily screamed my name, she trembled beneath me, and the pressure that had been building inside me for so long was finally released in a huge, earth-shattering, havoc-wreaking wave after wave of pleasure. Explosive currents raced through me, sending my lower body into convulsions from the most intense orgasm I'd ever had while I simultaneously witnessed Lex ride out her own lust-filled ecstasy.

Once we transitioned from climax into the aftermath, I collapsed on top of her with her warm breath wheezing rapidly against my ear. "Damn, Batman," she said, still trying to steady her breathing.

Her comment brought a smile to my face, but I didn't move from my spot. That place where my heart was aligned with hers and our bodies were still joined was my new favorite residence. I didn't want to ever leave.

But there was a knock on the door. "Cameron, are you in there?" The sound of my sister's voice slammed me back to reality. "If you are, check your phone."

I didn't want to answer the door or check my phone. Lex began to push me off her, but still held a beaming expression and released an appreciative sigh. "Just see what she wants."

I reluctantly pulled out of the best place I had ever been and quickly disposed of the condom. I located my shorts on the floor and dug my phone out of the deep pocket. We remained blissful without a stitch of clothing as Lex grabbed her phone from her purse, and we sat side by side on the bed, glancing at our screens.

Charlie: Where the hell did you two go?

Louis: We're ready to leave. Where should we meet you?

The text from Louis had been sent several minutes ago. I glanced over at Lex, and she quickly glimpsed at me before directing her gaze down and hitting buttons on her phone.

Alexis: You two should go ahead and take the car. We can always take the shuttle.

"So now I know you're in there." I guess my sister looked at her phone. "Maybe we'll see you later." Footsteps retreated away from our door, and we were alone again.

Charlie: I'm happy for you both. I love you guys [heart emoji]

Cam: See you later. No need to check up on us.

Charlie: [puking emoji]

Louis: Have fun.

Alexis: We intend to.

Charlie: [girl vomiting GIF]

Desiring a much-needed shower, and given that we were both already naked, we let the hot water spray on us and indulged in some heated passion while washing each other off. We ordered room service and didn't have clothes touch our bodies for the rest of the day.

13
ALEXIS

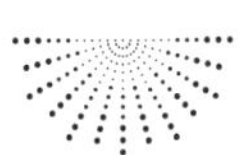

I felt like I'd been living in a dream for the last few weeks. School was back in session, so Cam didn't have to be at work so early in the mornings now that the sunrise sports practices were over. Louis had officially been living with Charlie since right before our Labor Day weekend getaway.

Cam and I talked about moving in together also. We'd spent every night together except the nights I worked for quite a while now. I liked having my own place, but I liked being with Cam even more. I guess I finally found what I was looking for my whole life. I had friends, a family, a job I was passionate about, and a kind, gentle, caring, wonderful man who loved me and treated me well.

Charlie insisted that we'd be sisters soon by marriage. I wasn't sure if or when we'd get married, but I already felt like I was a part of the Callahan family. Cam's mom had me calling her MommaRita now, and Cam's father didn't want to be referred to as anything but Dad, so that's how it had been at the family Sunday dinners. Dad made it known that he thought of me as one of his own children, just like Claudette, the twins, and Louis.

Even though I came into the relationship inexperienced, I was quickly converted into a woman who couldn't get enough of her man. Aside from the things he had taught me about love and kindness, he showed me desire and fevered passion as well. He made me feel beautiful and appreciated. Plus, he was sexy as hell. Most of the time, we couldn't keep our hands to ourselves.

Sometimes we engaged in traditional handholding. Sometimes we linked our thumbs and spread our fingers. Sometimes we gave each other a chaste kiss. And sometimes, we tried to rip each other's clothes off as fast as humanly possible. We managed to keep our PDA to PG-rated when in the presence of others, but when we were alone, it was another story. Sometimes we needed to sneak away for some privacy so we could engage in some good old-fashioned necking. I didn't have any idea if that was how a relationship was supposed to be, since he was my first boyfriend. If I could make one wish, it would be for Cam to be my last boyfriend, too.

He liked when I called him Batman. I guess it made him feel powerful or something. So I often used it when we are alone in the bedroom. Butterfly had become an endearing name to him, so he used it when he was trying to be sweet. His nickname for me still gave me gooseflesh. Of course, I loved when he called me Lex, especially in that deep, husky voice of his.

I hadn't had any more nightmares, and I hadn't had any more run-ins with my biological father, either. I also no longer carried a knife in my purse. I have heard people say you shouldn't lose your sense of self once you're in a relationship. I got that. I used to enjoy solitude, and I used to feel like I could take on the world without anyone standing in my way. It's not that I didn't feel that way anymore. I just didn't feel like I *needed* to take on the world on my own anymore. I had friends I could depend on and who cared about me. I felt like I didn't lose myself, but rather, I'd found myself. I was confident with who I was now and where I was going. I have also realized I wasn't alone.

Previously, I thought I wanted to be alone because all of the individuals in my life were terrible, and being alone rather than with them was so much better. Now I understood I just had the wrong people in my life. I wouldn't trade the Callahans for anything in the world. It wasn't better to be alone. It was better to be surrounded by good friends.

As for my mom, it'd been over five and a half years, and I hadn't heard from or seen her. I probably shouldn't say I didn't care, but she'd made her choice. She could've left with me that day all those years ago. She'd made the decision to stay with her boyfriend, rather than be with her daughter. That spoke volumes to me. Some women didn't have the opportunity to get out of the domestic violence cycle, but I was there giving her a hand. All she had to do was to take it. I had read the statistics, and I realized that it was extremely possible that she was no longer alive at this point. I did think it was better if I was left wondering. It made me feel better to be angry at her for abandoning me than to know that she had died at the hands of a jackass.

I hadn't lived in fear in a long time. In fact, it had been quite the opposite. I refused to be scared of anyone or anything since I ran away from home at sixteen. I hadn't allowed myself to feel vulnerable. However, I had managed to convince myself that letting men and women into my life would make me vulnerable to being hurt and manipulated. I was happily proven wrong on that front. I was glad that I was strong enough to trust that not all people were bad. I learned to see the good in others and actually believe it. Opening myself up to friends who cared about me had shown me true love and happiness.

EPILOGUE

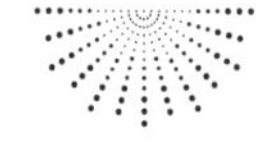

CAMERON

O*ne year later…*

Lex and I waited anxiously for Charlie and Louis to arrive at their surprise engagement party. Louis had texted me that they were on their way a few moments ago.

The couple walked into the restaurant hand in hand, and they were quickly ushered to the back room, where they were greeted with a loud shouting of *"Surprise!"* by our closest friends and family.

Charlie genuinely looked surprised and happy. She actually glowed in the presence of all the excitement. Louis wanted a private proposal, but he also wanted to tell everyone immediately afterward. So it made sense to invite everyone out to celebrate with them.

I, of course, greeted my sister and my best friend before the other guests. "I always knew you two would end up together." I clapped Louis on the back and gave Charlie a quick hug.

"Oh, you did not," she quipped at me. "You only recently become a gooey romantic after you started dating Alexis."

I shrugged and pulled Lex from the group walking close by. I smacked a loud kiss on my girlfriend's mouth, and she giggled.

"Congratulations. We're very happy for you," Lex said before I pulled her away.

We watched as Travis and Claudette approached them next. They had become part of our circle of friends over this last year. They had both said that their relationship was completely platonic, but I felt like something else might be developing there. They seemed to complement each other nicely. They both gave their congratulations to Charlie and Louis and then advanced to the seafood buffet the restaurant was famous for. Maybe once Travis was ready to move on, their relationship would evolve into something more, I thought to myself, as I watched them walk away together side by side.

Lex and I walked to the hallway near the restrooms. I would be proposing before too long. I didn't want to steal my sister's thunder, so I would wait a respectable amount of time. Maybe a week or two...

I would also make sure it was in a private setting. I didn't need the celebration with all my family and friends. I just needed my Butterfly. We could have our own private celebration.

We'd been living together for nearly nine months, so getting married was definitely the next step in our happily-ever-after life together. We were still young, but we were meant to be. We were Butterfly and Batman, and we would always be together.

ABOUT THE AUTHOR

Greenleigh lives on the Eastern Shore of Maryland with her husband and four children. Being an ER nurse for two decades and married to a firefighter, she writes stories about what she knows. Coffee and chocolate are everyday must haves in her life, but fishing and relaxing at the beach are her favorite pastimes.

After a pancreatic cancer diagnosis in 2019, Greenleigh began to check things off her bucket list—one of those things being "write a novel." Today she is healthy and continues to write whenever she can, so she can get the stories in her head down on paper. She is inspired by people that chase their dreams and is a firm believer in happily ever afters, so you will find her characters and their stories mirror these ideals.

GRATITUDES

Brian: You are the love of my life. Thank you for being by my side for all of life's ups and downs. You have always encouraged me to chase my dreams no matter how ambitious they were! You are the reason I can write about romance, because you show me every day

To my beta readers Christy and Tania: Thank you for reading the roughest of drafts and giving me honest feedback. You two are the best!

To my sister Anna: Thank you for reading this book and even managing to read the sex scenes this time around.

To Robin at *Wicked by Design Covers*: Thank you once again for creating a book cover that I absolutely adore!

To Eunice: Thank you for the coffee and the talk. You are amazing at what you do for women and children every day! I admire your strength, commitment, and advocacy to the vulnerable population you care for.

To Leddy: I don't even know what to say at this point. You are my dream-maker, my friend, my mentor, my role model, my idol. I didn't know when you showed up in my life you would make such an impact on me. My writing and I used to be trapped like a caterpillar in a cocoon, and you transformed my writing into a butterfly so I could fly. You will forever be my inspiration and my favorite author!

To my readers: Thank you for taking a chance on me. I have always believed that stories are written for other people to read, so I am extremely grateful to each of you that decided to read this one! I hope you enjoyed it! I really have enjoyed writing about the Callahans. I couldn't let the twins have their stories told without writing more about their sister. So I decided Claudette needed her own story too. I hope to release her book in Fall of 2021, so keep an eye out for it!

ALSO BY GREENLEIGH ADAMS

Love Burns

RESOURCES

Alexis was extremely fortunate to come away from the trauma of her childhood with minimal emotional scars. If you or someone you know is a victim of domestic violence, there is help available. You may call the **National Domestic Violence Hotline at 800-799-SAFE (7233)** Seven Days a week, 24 hours a day.

The trauma from childhood abuse can induce long-term manifestations of distress for victims, which ultimately affects their adult relationships.

How the Trauma of Childhood Abuse Affects Interpersonal Relationships, and How to Begin Healing highlights the long-term effects of the trauma of childhood abuse and how it affects individuals into adulthood. Blogs with survivor stories can also be reached at this site.

Adult survivors of childhood trauma: Complex trauma, complex needs provides a lot of insight on symptoms seen in survivors of childhood trauma. Some of these symptoms were emulated in Alexis's character (nightmares, flashbacks, fragmented memories from childhood, etc.)

Websites:

https://www.thehotline.org/

https://www.bridgestorecovery.com/blog/trauma-childhood-abuse-affects-interpersonal-relationships-begin-healing/

https://www1.racgp.org.au/ajgp/2020/july/adult-survivors-of-childhood-trauma

Made in the USA
Middletown, DE
29 July 2021